"You still don't believe I'm a genie, do you?" G.T. asked.

"Convince me," Hayley challenged boldly.

G.T. liked her. Out of the hundreds of people he'd worked for and had the pleasure of doing business with, she was by far the spunkiest, most compassionate and altogether sexiest woman he'd ever met.

It was too bad that he couldn't act on these feelings, he thought grumpily. But no. Rule three hundred eleven was not meant to be taken lightly. Those who broke this cardinal rule suffered grim consequences for their choice.

"You mean I've granted four out of your seven wishes so far and I haven't convinced you yet?" Sitting up straighter, he leaned toward her and whispered into her ear, "Tell me what else I can do."

Dear Reader,

What makes a man a SUPER FABULOUS FATHER? In bestselling author Lindsay Longford's *Undercover Daddy*, detective Walker Ford promises to protect a little boy with his life. Even though that means an undercover marriage to the child's mother—the woman he'd always loved but could never have...until now.

Book 2 of Silhouette's cross-line continuity miniseries, DADDY KNOWS LAST, continues with *Baby in a Basket* by award-winning author Helen R. Myers. A confirmed bachelor finds a baby on his doorstep—with a note claiming the baby is his!

In Carolyn Zane's *Marriage in a Bottle,* a woman is granted seven wishes by a very mysterious, very sexy stranger. And her greatest wish is to make him her husband....

How is a woman to win over a bachelor cowboy and his three protective little cowpokes? With lots of love—in *Cowboy at the Wedding* by Karen Rose Smith, book one of her new miniseries, THE BEST MEN.

Why does Laurel suddenly want to say "I do" to the insufferable—irresistible—man who broke her heart long ago? It's all in *The Honeymoon Quest* by Dana Lindsey.

All Tip wants is to be with single dad Rob Winfield and his baby daughter, but will her past catch up with her? Don't miss *Mommy for the Moment* by Lisa Kaye Laurel.

From classic love stories to romantic comedies to emotional heart tuggers, Silhouette Romance brings you six irresistible novels this month—and every month—by six talented authors. I hope you treasure each and every one.

Regards,

Melissa Senate
Senior Editor

Please address questions and book requests to:
Silhouette Reader Service
U.S.: 3010 Walden Ave., P.O. Box 1325, Buffalo, NY 14269
Canadian: P.O. Box 609, Fort Erie, Ont. L2A 5X3

MARRIAGE IN A BOTTLE

Carolyn Zane

Silhouette
ROMANCE™
Published by Silhouette Books
America's Publisher of Contemporary Romance

For Melissa Jeglinski, editor extraordinaire without whom my books
would be ful of reely bad speling and worser grammer. Thank you
for your talent, creativity and friendship.

And for my father, Douglas Tope, for his willingness to
share his wild ideas and terrific sense of humor.
This book is more his baby than mine.

Also, special thanks to the Lord,
for the fun and magic you add to my life.

 SILHOUETTE BOOKS

ISBN 0-373-19170-7

MARRIAGE IN A BOTTLE

Copyright © 1996 by Carolyn Suzanne Pizzuti

All rights reserved. Except for use in any review, the reproduction
or utilization of this work in whole or in part in any form by any
electronic, mechanical or other means, now known or hereafter
invented, including xerography, photocopying and recording, or in
any information storage or retrieval system, is forbidden without
the written permission of the editorial office, Silhouette Books,
300 East 42nd Street, New York, NY 10017 U.S.A.

All characters in this book have no existence outside the imagination of
the author and have no relation whatsoever to anyone bearing the same
name or names. They are not even distantly inspired by any individual
known or unknown to the author, and all incidents are pure invention.

This edition published by arrangement with Harlequin Books S.A.

® and TM are trademarks of Harlequin Books S.A., used under license.
Trademarks indicated with ® are registered in the United States Patent
and Trademark Office, the Canadian Trade Marks Office and in other
countries.

Printed in U.S.A.

CAROLYN ZANE

lives with her husband, Matt, in the rolling countryside near Portland, Oregon's Willamette River. Their menagerie, which includes two cats, Jazz and Blues, and a golden retriever, Bob Barker, was recently joined by baby daughter, Madeline. Although Carolyn spent months poring over the baby-name books, looking for just the right name for their firstborn, her husband was adamant about calling her Madeline. "After all, Matt plus Carolyn equals Madeline." How could she resist such logic?

So, when Carolyn is not busy changing Maddie, or helping her husband renovate their rambling one-hundred-plus-year-old farmhouse, she makes time to write.

Dear Reader,

In Carolyn Zane's exciting and hilarious *Marriage in a Bottle,* the heroine meets a handsome genie who grants her seven wishes. Read on to find out just how much fun and romance those wishes lead to.

But before you turn the page, take this opportunity to put yourself in the place of the heroine. Use the following list to write down what you'd wish for if a sexy stranger said he'd be able to grant you *anything.* (Just remember, no wishing for more wishes!)

MY WISH LIST:

1._____

2._____

3._____

4._____

5._____

6._____

7._____

Prologue

"Hayley, if you keep napping on your keyboard that way, you're going to end up looking like a waffle. Do you want me to get you a blanket and pillow?"

Hayley Douglas opened one eye and trained it listlessly on Mercedes, her closest friend and co-worker at Technolabs, Inc. Heaving a great dispirited sigh, she pushed herself away from her computer and touched her cheek. Mercedes was right. There was a definite keyboard pattern imprinted on her face. Oh, well. She shoved a seemingly endless mountain of files out of the way and, resting her elbows on the desk, rubbed her throbbing temples.

She hated her job.

"Hey." Mercedes' heavy East Coast accent whined above the workaday hubbub of the massive Data Processing department where, for the last four years, she'd shared a cubicle with Hayley. "You should look alive, you know? You don't want to get sacked on your birthday."

Hayley focused a bleary eye in the direction of the nagging voice and shrugged. "Why not? It might be the best present I get, considering I could be asleep and still perform this daily grind.'' She trailed her fingers dully across her keyboard as she spoke. ''Come to think of it,'' she said, closing her eyes and letting her head loll back against her ergonomically correct chair, ''I could be in a coma with no discernible brainwave activity, and still do this job.''

Mercedes snorted. ''You're just all bent out of shape because you have to work on your birthday.''

''No,'' Hayley smiled wanly. ''I'm just bent out of shape because I have to work *here.* I'm twenty-seven years old for crying in the night, and still in the Data Processing pool. What am I doing here?''

''Earning a living. And if you want to keep earning a living, snap out of it,'' Mercedes advised, fluffing her spiky, henna-red hair. ''It's almost time.''

''For what?'' Hayley mumbled, glancing at her watch. Quitting time was light years away. Sighing, she watched Mercedes outline her mouth with a bright lip pencil in the reflection of her monitor.

Mercedes shook her head. ''Don't you ever read your memos?''

Stretching, Hayley recrossed her legs and dangled her pump from her toe. ''Why should I? You're only too happy to keep me up-to-the-minute on the office rumor mill. Besides—'' her tone was petulant ''—today is my birthday. I shouldn't have to do anything I don't want to.''

Unfortunately, she thought, feeling sorry for herself, she wasn't going to get to do anything she wanted to, either. Everyone it seemed, was busy. Too busy to help her celebrate her twenty-seventh birthday. It was uncanny how her friends and family had all but forgotten her special day. For pity's sake, even her own parents were leaving town for the weekend.

It was then that it dawned on her. Maybe someone had decided to throw a surprise party for her. That would explain why everyone was so busy tonight. Yeah... The more she thought about it, the more likely it seemed. A surprise party. A shiver of anticipation skittered down her spine.

Then again, the last time she'd been sure someone was throwing a surprise party for her she'd ended up disappointed. Her mother had honestly believed that she would prefer a quiet little ice cream social to a big surprise slumber party.

"Mmm." Mercedes blotted her lips on the memo in question, then passed it to her friend. "You might want to make an exception and read this, birthday girl."

"Gee, Mercedes," she groused, trying to make out the words beneath the various lip prints. "Attention Data Processing Department. This Friday, July 7, our new general manager, Grant Thompson, will be touring the building. Please have all areas tidy and presentable. Coffee cups should be rinsed and stored in the lounge. Work stations and monitors must be dusted and polished. All personal effects not pertaining to the office are to be stored in drawers for the duration." Hayley opened her desk drawer and swept her plastic plant inside. "Wouldn't want to offend His Majesty," she said grumpily.

"C'mon," Mercedes coaxed, tossing a comb in Hayley's direction. "Don't you at least want to primp a little? What if he's cute?"

"Oh, sure. Cute." Hayley drew her brows together and tugged the comb halfheartedly through her wild mop of blond waves. "Just like all the other fine specimens here at Technolabs." She wrinkled her delicate nose in disdain and tossed the comb back to her friend.

Mercedes deftly caught it with her makeup bag. "Okay for you," she droned through her nose. "If he's cute, I get him."

"You have a boyfriend."

"True, my Owen's the best. But hey, I'm always lookin' to trade up." Mercedes wiggled her finely plucked brows.

Pulling another file off the stack in her In basket, Hayley began to type halfheartedly. "You know he's going to be old, fat and bald, just like all the other guys around here."

Mercedes rummaged through her desk drawer till she found an aging magazine and rubbed her wrists vigorously on a perfume ad. "Big deal. My Owen's losing his hair, and he's still sexy." She dropped the magazine into the waste basket and regarded her co-worker. "You know, Hayley, that's your problem. You're too picky. That's why you don't have a date for your birthday tonight. You've got guys falling all over you... all the women in this department could cheerfully strangle you because you're the most gorgeous woman here at Technolabs... and you have a wonderful personality to boot. But you're the only one without a steady guy. I don't get it."

"Is wanting someone born in the same century as me asking too much?" Hayley pursed her lips. "Just because I won't date Freddy the Frantic from Accounting or Walt the Weirdo from Human Resources, doesn't mean I'm too picky," she said defensively. "They just don't happen to have the qualities I'm looking for in a man." She tossed the document she'd completed into her Out basket. "Or in a rock, for that matter," she muttered under her breath.

Mercedes spun in her chair to face her computer. "So," she ordered, as her fingers flew across her keyboard. "Tell me about these special qualities you're looking for in a man."

Changing screens, Hayley began a new document. "Well," she mused aloud, "there are four basic qualities that I find really attractive in a man."

"And these are?"

"First of all, I don't happen to think looks are all that important." Frowning thoughtfully, Hayley let her fingers rest lightly on her keyboard.

Mercedes laughed. "Oh, right."

"No, really." She tipped her chin to her shoulder and looked over at Mercedes. "I think I'd much rather have a man with a sense of humor than someone with flawless looks. It's what's inside that counts," she said with conviction.

Shrugging, Mercedes tossed her head. "Whatever revs your engine, hon. I happen to like drop-dead gorgeous, but hey, if you prefer ugly and funny, who am I to quibble?"

Ignoring her, Hayley continued. "Second, I want someone who's self-confident, no matter what he looks like," she said, drawing her lower lip into her mouth in concentration. "Let's see, now. Third, I want someone with the creativity to make something of himself, regardless of his station in life. And lastly, someone with a lust for life... a sense of adventure."

Mercedes grinned at her screen. "Finding a guy who fits all of these requirements could be tough."

Hayley lifted her shoulders lightly. "He doesn't have to have all of them. Heck, if I could find a single man with just *one* of these qualities, I'd be thrilled. I'm not greedy."

"You just described my Owen," Mercedes chuckled. "Humorous, self-confident, creative, adventurous and funny looking. Tell you what. If I don't like his folks tonight, you can have him."

Hayley shook her head. "Would you relax? They're going to love you." All week long, Mercedes had done nothing but chatter on about how nervous she was to finally meet Owen's parents.

Hayley suddenly found it very interesting that this big event just happened to coincide with her birthday. She wondered absently if this whole story about meeting Owen's parents was just an elaborate excuse Mercedes had trumped up to throw her off the surprise party trail. It was always so hard to tell with Mercedes. She had a real poker face.

"You still goin' to the beach after work today?" Mercedes' eyes didn't waver from the screen.

"Yeah. Why? You want to come for awhile?"

"Nah. I gotta go get ready for my date." Mercedes pitched another file into her Out basket. "I was just curious, that's all. Just wondered what you had planned, you know, to do for your birthday. You're goin' to the usual spot?"

Hayley arched a thoughtful brow. What was this, the grand inquisition? Then a slow smile tipped her lips as the idea struck that perhaps Mercedes was throwing her a party down at the *beach*. It was a long shot, but she decided to play dumb just in case and waved an airy hand. "Yep, I think I'll be down at the same spot, where we always go, you know, that spot right next to the end of that big log?"

"Oh." Mercedes grinned. "That's an excellent choice."

"I sure wish you could come with me."

"Me, too." Mercedes was contrite. "Normally I'd love to go out on the town with you tonight, but this thing with Owen's folks could be serious. You understand."

"Sure. I understand." Hayley tried to swallow past the sudden thickening in her throat. She understood that Mercedes was right. Everyone on this planet, with the painful exception of herself, seemed to be involved with someone. Exhaling drearily at her computer screen, she doggedly began to type. She was another year older, with no decent man in her foreseeable future. She didn't feel like celebrating. She felt like screaming.

And this job. Lordy, how she hated this job.

Propping her elbows on her desk, she cradled her head in her hands and rubbed her weary eyes. The tedium was killing her. She was twenty-seven years old and still wasting her life in this nowhere department, working for this nowhere company. Sighing, she closed her eyes and allowed her head to thud dramatically on her desktop. Unfortunately, it was true.

She really could do this job in her sleep.

Chapter One

"Okay, so where is everybody?" Hayley muttered lazily as she sat on her towel in the warm slanting rays of the afternoon sun. Peering over the edge of her sunglasses, she squinted up and down the beach for signs of her approaching party.

But so far, the only sign of anything even remotely resembling a party, was a group of teens who were horsing around off in the distance. She'd been waiting in the usual spot—leaning against the old log as promised—for nearly two hours. The sun hovered low on the horizon, causing white diamonds to dance on the ocean's surface. Gulls dipped and wheeled against the splendorous, multicolored Pacific sky.

Rolling onto her side, Hayley stretched languorously and began to push some sand into a pile and shape a crude castle. The hot sand was comforting as she let it sift through her fingers. She loved the beach. Every Friday for as long as she could remember, she and Mercedes would spend the afternoon together after work, on the sandy shores of this secluded section of Southern California beach, and watch the world go by. Every Friday, that is, except for today. Her birthday.

So, Hayley thought, feeling somewhat despondent and very much alone, it seemed that she could scratch beach party off her list of possible ways to celebrate the passage of another year. She worked for a while building an authentic-looking fortress that she wished—in a fit of melancholy whimsy—housed her knight in shining armor. If only life were that simple.

What a way to spend her birthday. Playing fairy princess in the sand like a little kid. Disgusted with herself, she wondered when she was ever going to grow up and get on with her life. Get married and have a couple of children. Like everyone else.

Then again, she thought in her own defense, it wasn't as if she'd been actively avoiding these things. In order to get married and have a couple of children, one needed a man. Nothing fancy. Just some nice guy with a few decent attributes. Unfortunately, all of these men were taken. And the few nut cases she worked with that were single didn't bear thinking about.

Sitting up straight, she began to fashion a moat in the sand around her castle with a small stick of driftwood. She guessed if she was ever going to find what she was looking for, she was going to have to actively pursue it. She needed to get aggressive. Viciously digging the moat with her stick, she made a vow as she sent the sand flying. This would be the last time she celebrated her birthday alone. With a determined set to her jaw, she decided that this time next year she'd be married, or engaged, or at the very least, involved—or know the reason why she wasn't. The fact that she was alone on this birthday was really nobody's fault but her own.

Maybe Mercedes had been right, she decided, beginning to plan her strategy. Maybe she was too picky. Well—she

tossed her hair over her shoulder and then picked a strand
of seaweed out of her moat—if she had to lower her standards, then so be it. After all, it wasn't as if she was perfect. Why should she expect her mate to be? That decision
made, Hayley felt a lot better. Determined. Energized.
Empowered.

"Hear me roar!" she shouted forcefully, knowing her
corny plan might not turn out the way she expected, but
glad at least that she now had a goal. She attacked the moat
with renewed energy. "Hey," she murmured as she stabbed
into an obstruction that was interfering with the perfect
circle of her moat. "What's this?" Digging around the object, she finally managed to pry it out of the ground.

It was a bottle of some sort, covered with barnacles, and
bits and pieces of seaweed. The shape was very unusual,
and, running her fingers over the rough surface, Hayley fell
into a fanciful muse about its origin. Had it washed up on
this beach after having traveled a great distance? Maybe
from a foreign country or ship?

Hayley held the bottle up in the fading glow of the afternoon sun and studied it. It sure looked old. She'd never
seen anything quite like it. Settling herself back on her
beach towel, she gave it a shake. "Sounds like there's
something inside," she whispered, looking around for a
tool that would help her open it. Grabbing a sandal, she
beat on the funny-looking stopper, but it didn't budge.

"Nope." She sighed. "That won't work. Hmm, what's
in there?" she wondered as a surge of excitement traveled
down her spine. Maybe it was something valuable. Hayley
poked at the stopper with her car keys to no avail. And,
when her back teeth began to ache, she decided that biting
it off wasn't a good idea, either. Hayley rubbed her jaw.
There had to be a better way.

Glancing around, she spotted a forked root at the end of
the large log she was leaning against. Scrambling quickly up
the smooth surface of the old driftwood, she wedged the

stopper securely at the base of the roots and, grasping the crusty bottle, leaned back for all she was worth.

She tugged. She grunted. She turned red in the face. And finally with a sharp pop the stopper shot out of the bottle, releasing a stream of odious gray smoke and sending Hayley tumbling off the log and onto her bottom. Shaking her head, she blinked and held her breath to avoid the bizarre pollution that was filling the air. When it had finally fizzled out, Hayley sat up and burst out laughing at the spectacle she must have made.

"Boy, howdy! Smells like ten-thousand-year-old sweat socks," she said, waving her hands to clear the air. Standing, she brushed the sand out of her eyes. Once the last of the smoke had dissipated, she retrieved the bottle from where it had landed on the ground and peered into its dark recesses.

"Wheew. Make that twenty thousand," she murmured, curiously sniffing the dank interior. "What's this?" She fished a crinkly brown piece of parchment paper from the neck of the bottle and, unrolling it, held the small note up to the light in order to better inspect it. The writing on the paper looked like some sort of Egyptian hieroglyphics.

She peered intently at the strange markings. Around the ragged edges, there appeared to be a series of little stars and moons and planets inscribed. The center of the small page contained a circle of what looked to Hayley like the letter L. Seven little Ls around one big one.

"L... What could that stand for?" she wondered aloud. Maybe they could tell her what it was down at the museum. Hayley tucked the scrap of paper into her purse with the bottle and, glancing up, noticed that the group of teenagers off in the distance was packing up and preparing to leave.

Well, she decided, suddenly feeling bereft now that even the teens were deserting her, I may as well head home, too. She'd had her excitement for the day. Slowly, she shook the

sand out of her towel and folded it into a neat square. If she
hurried, she could rent a video and make it home in time to
order a pizza and do her nails. Then, for a rousing grand
finale, she could catch up on her beauty sleep in her recliner.

Some birthday this had turned out to be. A smelly old
bottle and a vow to marry the first Tom, Dick or Harry who
would have her. How had it come to this?

She slogged through the sand across the beach to the
parking lot, where she unlocked her aging compact car and
tossed her towel and beach bag into the trunk. Sliding into
the blistering interior, she wished she'd taken time to pull
her shorts on over her swimsuit, as the seat belt branded a
painful design on her thigh. After quickly unrolling the
window and gasping for air, she jammed her key into the
ignition. The sooner she could get Old Trusty here started,
the sooner she could cool down under the air conditioner.

The only problem was, Old Trusty wouldn't start. No,
the only reaction Old Trusty gave to her repeated attempts
at starting the engine was a feeble buzz and what sounded
like a couple of dying gasps. Sagging in frustration against
the searing-hot steering wheel, she groaned. The battery. Or
the fan belt. Or the water pump. Or any of a dozen other
mysterious auto parts she'd been neglecting.

Damn. Hayley jumped out of her oven on wheels and
angrily kicked the tire. "Why me?" she moaned, realizing
too late that kicking the tire was only a good idea when one
was wearing shoes. "Oww." Standing on one foot, she
cradled her throbbing toe and glanced around the deserted
parking lot. "Aw, for the love of Mike. I don't want to walk
all the way home, carrying all this stuff," she cried, sagging miserably against Old Trusty. "Damn," she whimpered, fighting the frustrating urge to lie down on the
ground and throw a tantrum over life's little injustices. "I
just...wish I had a ride home." This was her birthday.
Couldn't anything go right?

Sounds of a car skidding to a stop behind her brought her head up. The sputtering motor of a beat-up yellow taxi idled noisily as one of the most fantastically handsome men Hayley had ever laid eyes on threw open his door, leapt out and strode over to where she stood.

"Hi, ma'am," he greeted her, grinning rakishly. "You must be the one with car trouble. I got the call." A look that could pass for appreciation flashed briefly into his eyes as they skimmed her brightly colored swimsuit.

Setting her wounded foot gingerly on the ground, Hayley wrapped her arms around her waist and stared at him. "What call?" she asked, perplexed.

The cabdriver shrugged artlessly. "Uh, well, you know. The call for a ride?" Appealing smile lines bracketed his sensuous lips as he lifted them to expose a set of perfect, snow-white teeth. Folding his arms across his broad, muscular chest, he stood with his legs spread slightly apart and nodded sagely at her car. "You are having car trouble, aren't you?"

"Uh..." Dumbfounded, Hayley tried to swallow past the sudden dryness in her throat. She made a mental note to think about adding good looks to her list of requirements for the man of her dreams. "Yes, I am, but...I didn't...uh..."

"Better get going, then." He lifted a casual thumb in the direction of his cab. "Meter's running." Another sexy, devastating grin.

"Yes. Well. I'll just get my...things...." Hayley, unable to tear her eyes off this cab-driving deity, backed up toward the trunk of her car.

His hair was the color of midnight, and his eyes—as far as she could tell under his lazily hooded gaze—were just as dark. It was hard to say, but she guessed him to be somewhere near her age. Maybe a little older. He exuded a power that she'd never experienced before in the presence of any other male. A power so intense, it seemed almost to drag her under its spell. She shook her head. She'd obviously spent too much time listening to Mercedes blather on about good-looking men. It was beginning to interfere with her objectivity.

Quickly unlocking her trunk, she grabbed her shoes and beach bag, slammed the lid shut and pulled an extra-large T-shirt on over her skimpy suit, all the while wondering how this guy had known she needed a cab.

Had Mercedes sent him? Must have, as she was the only one who knew that Hayley'd still be here. Maybe Mercedes had arranged for a surprise party at her house, and was growing worried since she hadn't shown up yet.

Smiling at the thought of Mercedes' sweet gesture, Hayley went all warm and fuzzy inside. Her trustworthy friend must have known how her car had been acting up. Of course, that had to be it. This guy had to be legitimate. After all, the cab company logo was stretched tautly across his impressive chest, and the car certainly looked like a cab. Chances were she didn't have anything to worry about.

That decided, Hayley allowed him to lead her to the vehicle and tuck her and her possessions inside before he hopped into the driver's seat and dove headlong into the Friday afternoon rush hour.

"So," the handsome cabby asked as he adjusted his rearview mirror to better see her. "Where to?" His dark eyes crinkled at the corners.

"Oh, uh..." Good question, Hayley thought, her gaze locked in a mesmerizing grip with his. Gracious. Those eyes could drive all rational thought from her mind, even from the reflection of a crazily angled mirror. "Seventh and Elm. On the hill."

"Gotcha."

And how. Then, feeling as if he could read her thoughts, Hayley averted her eyes and glanced around the interior of the ratty cab. What was a guy who looked like him doing driving a cab? He should be starring in some sort of romantic movie, or modeling clothes for an elite agency. Maybe he just drove a cab to make ends meet while he searched for work. A lot of people in Southern California did that.

"Northeast?" he asked, shooting her a quizzical glance.

"Uh . . . yeah."

Tugging on the wheel, he rounded a corner and headed toward her neighborhood. "My name's GT," he offered, then waited for her to respond.

Hayley wet her lips. "Hello, GT." She wondered if he could hear the ridiculous pitter-pat of her heart above the roar of the old engine. "I'm Hayley."

"That's a pretty name," he commented, throwing them into a faster-moving lane of traffic. "Reminds me of the comet." His eyes crinkled again as he darted a quick glance at her, then back at the road.

Ridiculously, Hayley felt herself blush at the compliment. She'd heard it a million times before, but he made it sound somehow . . . wonderful. "Thank you," she managed to squeak as he ground into low and proceeded up the hill.

He handled the old taxi easily, coaxing it through the traffic as if it were the finest foreign import. Something about his self-confident air gave her the feeling that he could do many things very well. She attempted to clear her throat of the awkward mass that had lodged there, and glanced out the window. As much as she'd love to begin her assertiveness training on this guy, she couldn't think of a single thing to say. Luckily, he took care of that little problem for her.

"Car trouble, huh?" He shook his head, and Hayley couldn't help but notice the way his thick raven hair shimmered in the magical afternoon twilight. Clearing her throat again, she tore her eyes away and stared out the window as the familiar landscape rushed by.

Deciding that there was no time like the present to think about finding that future soul mate, she stumbled head-long into the art of conversation. "Yes," she said gaily, striving to sound upbeat about her broken car. "I think it's the carburetor. Or the fuel pump."

"Oh, well—" he lifted his broad shoulders in sympathy "—luckily those can be fixed. It's not the end of the world."

Hayley sighed, relaxing against the feeling of easy ca-maraderie he exuded. "True, but it couldn't have hap-pened at a worse time."

Slowing, GT pulled to a stop at a traffic light and glanced back at her. "Why's that?"

The sparks that seemed to fairly crackle from his onyx eyes had her catching her breath as she stared, mesmerized at his profile.

"I...it's my birthday," Hayley admitted, feeling slightly dazed and wondering why it was always so easy to tell complete strangers about life's little details. It wasn't as if he cared. Then again, it might make a nifty little ice break-er.

"Really?" His eyes flashed into hers. "Happy birth-day."

"Thanks." She smiled. Wow. He sounded as though he cared.

"So, how are you going to celebrate the occasion of your birth?" he asked, shifting through the gears and easing the car up to speed as the light turned green.

Dropping her hands into her lap, she quickly shook her head. "I don't have plans. Everyone I know is busy. Even my folks are going out of town this weekend." Hayley pushed the heavy blond curtain of her hair away from her face and exhaled sadly. "I just wish I didn't have to cook dinner. Cooking for one is such a bummer."

"Oh, yeah," GT agreed, "I'll grant you that. I'm the same way myself."

Angling her head, she caught his eye in the rearview mirror. "I thought about taking myself out to dinner, but I think that would only exaggerate the fact that everyone I know and love forgot me today." Looking away, she winced at how maudlin she sounded. Good heavens, she hoped he didn't think she was trying to wrangle a dinner invitation out of him. It's just that there was something about him. Something that made her feel as though she could bare her soul to him.

He nodded, his eyes back on the road ahead. "It's like that at the movies, too, don't you think? You can't help but feel like everyone's staring at you, wondering why you don't have any friends."

"Yes!" Hayley giggled. He knew. Although, she found that hard to believe. A Greek god like himself must have women crawling all over him at the movies and everywhere else.

GT pulled onto the palm-lined Seventh Street where she lived, slowed and glanced at her in the rearview mirror. "House number?"

"Seven seventy-seven." She pointed up toward the end of the street. "On the corner there."

Nodding, he pulled to a stop in front of her small Spanish-style bungalow. "Here you go."

So soon? Hayley mused, vaguely depressed that her visit with the dazzlingly fetching GT had come to an end.

"Great," she said, hopping out to the street and digging through her purse for the fare.

"Oh, that's not necessary." GT grinned and waved her money away. "Happy birthday."

Hayley dropped her hand and, leaning down, smiled through the window at him. How sweet. He was as nice as he was good-looking. "Thanks, I really appreciate that," she breathed, and, unable to think of anything else to say, waved awkwardly and backed up onto the curb.

Another potential soul mate down the drain, she thought, filled with frustration as she watched him pull away. What would Mercedes have done in this situation? Would she have invited him inside? Given him her card? Clubbed him over the head and dragged him by the hair into her cave?

Hayley sighed and turned toward her house. It was clear she would have to be better prepared next time opportunity knocked.

GT watched her grow smaller in his rearview mirror after he'd returned her cheerful wave. Man, he mused, humming along with a tune on the radio, she was a knockout. Just like something out of the swimsuit edition of *Sports Illustrated*. For once he'd been glad that his engine idled so noisily, and he hoped that the clatter had disguised his unprofessional—and involuntary—groan of appreciation when he'd first laid eyes on her. What a doll.

It was so nice to get a job where the client was as sweet as she was beautiful. In his time, he'd worked for all kinds, but never for someone who had him breathing so hard over a simple smile.

"Oh, hello, dear."

"Mom! What are you doing here?" Hayley asked, surprised to find her mother, Celeste Douglas, standing in her living room. It was for exactly this reason that she had deliberately forgotten to supply her folks with a spare key, she thought in irritation as she watched the older woman dust and rearrange her coffee table.

So—she wondered as she dumped her beach paraphernalia on her sofa and turned to look expectantly at her mother—how had she gotten inside? For heaven's sake, if Mom could break in, anyone could.

"Well, darling, I just stopped by to wish you a happy birthday since your father and I are leaving town tonight and we'll miss celebrating your special day." Celeste crossed to the sofa and began to tidy up her daughter's beach supplies.

"Mom," Hayley cried in exasperation as her mother sorted her beach towel and work clothes into differently colored piles, "you don't have to do that."

"Oh, it's no trouble." Celeste beamed. "It's the least I could do considering it's your birthday."

Hayley sighed. It was no use. She may as well give up and enjoy it. "Mom, how did you get in here?" she asked, snagging her khaki shorts from the darks pile and pulling them on over her suit. Flopping down into her recliner, she looked up at her mother.

"Your cook let me in."

"My *cook?*" Hayley frowned. Maybe she should open the windows. Her mother had obviously been breathing in too much furniture polish.

"Yes. He's out back heating up the grill. By the way—" Celeste wiggled her eyebrows up and down "—wherever did you get him? He's positively gorgeous! Captivating! And the smells in the kitchen . . . My goodness, I wish your father could cook like that." Frowning, she crossed back over to the coffee table and reached for her purse and car keys. "Well, anyway," her mother said, shooting her a conspiratorial wink, "I guess I won't worry about you not having any fun on your birthday. I have to get going. Your father and I should be back on Monday. Have a lovely time, dear."

"Mom, I . . ." Hayley began, but her mother seemed to be in an unusual rush. With a breezy kiss on her daughter's cheek, Celeste was gone.

Hayley stood at her living room window, watching her mother pull away from the curb, and wondered why her mother had been under the impression she had a cook.

And then . . . she wondered why she could smell the various aromas of garlic and onions—and was that baking bread?—coming from the direction of her kitchen.

But most of all, she wondered why it sounded like some-one was humming. From inside the house, no less. A slow smile began to spread across her face. Had Mercedes thrown her a surprise party, after all? Tucking her large T-shirt into the waistband of her shorts, she attempted to make herself presentable. Then, after pinching some roses into her cheeks and inspecting the state of her hair in the hallway mirror, she decided she'd pass.

Rushing toward the back of her house, Hayley came to a screeching halt as she reached her kitchen door.

For there, wearing a white paper chef's hat and rapidly chopping vegetables on her butcher's block, was the in-credibly handsome taxi driver. And, he was alone.

Chapter Two

"Hi," GT said, pinning her with a sexy, lazy grin. "You do like salmon, I hope." He stopped chopping and wiped his hands on a dish towel.

"Well, yes... I, uh," Hayley stammered, staring at him in shock. "How did you get in here?" She glanced around her sparkling, sunny white kitchen, looking for warning signs. Signs that he'd broken and entered. However, unless she counted the fact that her dishes were done and put away, and several new bags of groceries graced her counters and cabinets, nothing appeared to have been violated.

"Your mom let me in," he explained, and, holding his finger to his perfectly sculpted lips, very slowly and carefully opened her oven and peered inside. Seeming to decide that everything was going well, he cautiously shut the door and turned to face her. "Soufflé. Can't be too careful." A slow grin tugged at his mouth.

Her mother had let him in? That didn't add up. Celeste said that *he* had let *her* in, hadn't she? Then it dawned on her. Her birthday. Of course. That wacky Mercedes. This had to be some kind of birthday thing. It only made sense, considering she'd never heard of a soufflé-baking, salmon-grilling burglar. Especially not one who cleaned up after himself. She battled down her smile, trying to appear nonchalant. As though this kind of thing happened every day.

"So, you can make a soufflé? When you're not driving a cab, you cater dinner parties?" she asked, coming into the kitchen and sitting down on one of the stools at the island counter. If no one was going to tell her what was going on, she would be only too happy to play twenty questions with this Adonis look-alike. Mercedes must be behind this. From the looks of things, her mother, too. Well, she'd go along with it. Why not? After all, it beat eating pizza alone on her birthday.

"I do whatever the client wishes."

The client? She was a client? She smiled. "Whatever I wish?"

GT tossed her an easy answering smile that she was sure had done some kind of nuclear damage to her larger internal organs. "Whatever."

"Well," Hayley said, reaching out to snag an olive from the relish tray, "I'd sure like to know how you got back to my house so fast after dropping me off."

Sprawling lazily over the island's countertop toward her, GT pulled off his chef's hat and waggled a teasing finger. "That wasn't asked in the form of a wish, but, since it's your birthday and since I have to tell you, anyway, I'll go easy on you."

Brows drawn together in confusion, Hayley lifted her heavy tresses off her face. *What was he talking about?*

GT pushed himself away from the counter, sauntered over to the refrigerator and removed a bottle of wine. A very old, very strange-looking bottle of wine. He opened it, poured a small amount of the liquid into a long-stemmed glass, and handed it to her. "Hope you like this, it was a good year. Believe it or not, the ancient Egyptians could stomp a mean grape.''

Hayley took the glass and felt giddy bubbles, like the ones in the glass, rise into her throat. He had an appealing sense of humor. Strange, but appealing. Taking a tentative sip, she proclaimed, ''It's good.''

GT's dark eyes forked at the corners. ''Good.'' Crossing the room, he pulled open the bottom half of the Dutch door that led to her backyard and motioned for her to follow. ''Come on out here and keep me company,'' he said over his shoulder. ''I want to check the coals.''

Hopping off the stool, Hayley mutely followed the taxi-driver-turned-gourmet-chef to her back patio, unable to tear her eyes away from his retreating form. Approaching the smoking grill, he moved with an athletic grace that reminded Hayley of the easy, swaying gate of a wild animal. Narrow in the hips, long in the leg, broad in the shoulder, he was the stuff of young girls' fantasies. What in heaven's name was he doing cooking dinner for her? Surely he had better things to do on a Friday night.

She sat on one of the brightly flowered chairs of her patio set and watched him while she sipped at her glass of wine. This was the life. Whoever thought up this surprise had a lot of class, she thought contentedly. Apparently satisfied that the coals were coming along nicely, GT wandered over and took the chair next to Hayley's.

''So, GT.'' Hayley ran her forefinger around the rim of her glass and regarded him with interest. ''You never did answer my question.''

GT cleared his throat and watched her bring the glass to her fabulous, kissable-looking lips. ''Uh, what was the question?'' he asked, dragging his eyes away from her mouth and up to her eyes. He knew it wouldn't do to let the client see even a glimmer of attraction. It went against the rules. Although, in this case, he found the rules somewhat irritating. Hayley was by far the most beautiful woman he'd ever had the good fortune to work for.

Long, wavy hair of spun gold that hung halfway down her back. A body that any self-respecting belly dancer would kill for. And a face that would launch ships. GT felt his pulse pick up speed and swallowed, battling this primal reaction to Hayley. He was working for her. He had to get a grip.

"How did you get back to my house so fast?"

Ah. Yes. Plowing his hands through his hair, he glanced around her tidy little yard. He hated this part of his job. The part where he had to tell the client who he was. They usually never took it for face value and had a little fun. No. Usually, they overanalyzed and questioned until all the joy was gone. Oh, well. That wasn't his problem. That was the boss's problem. He had a job to do. And, whether or not it made any sense half the time, it wasn't for him to worry about.

"I got back to your house so fast because . . ." His eyes shot to hers, and he could almost feel himself begin to fall into their sapphire depths. "Because I'm your genie."

Her eyes widened perceptibly. "My *genie?*" She grinned.

Hmm. This was not as hard as he'd figured. Usually this was where the client screamed, called him a liar and told him to get lost. Hayley on the other hand, was smiling. And what a smile, he thought, basking under the brilliance that was surely brighter than any star that the mundane-by-comparison galaxy had to offer.

"Yes. You've got some wishes to use, and your wish is, basically, my command."

"My . . . genie." She sounded skeptical.

Okay, maybe she wasn't a believer yet, but at least she wasn't calling the cops. "Yep."

Hayley laughed. She had a great laugh, he mused, as she held her wineglass up to him in salute. Like wind chimes dancing on a spring breeze. It stirred something elemental in his gut.

"And I suppose you're here to grant me my birthday wish?" she asked, laughing again. She took another sip of the wine. This must be pretty powerful stuff, she thought, enjoying the fruity flavor. Because she could have sworn that GT had told her he was her genie. Well, she decided, watching as he leaned back and made himself comfortable in his chair, if it wasn't the wine playing tricks on her, it had to be Mercedes. What a crazy birthday present. A genie in blue jeans. Ha. Nice touch. "And I can wish for anything I want?"

"Anything." GT nodded.

Hayley watched him pull his tennis-shoe-clad foot up over his knee and let his wrists dangle over his leg as he settled into his seat. His self-confidence didn't seem overblown at such an outrageous promise. However, he didn't seem to have any doubts, either. It almost seemed as if he were telling her the truth. But that was impossible. How could he grant her anything? He was probably banking on the fact that she would ask him for a kiss, or a date, or any number of easy-to-provide wishes.

Too bad that in her, she thought, amused, he'd met his match. She would have a little fun here, and make him work for the money Mercedes had no doubt forked over. Then it dawned on her that, knowing Mercedes, he was probably a stripper.

She clutched the arms of her patio chair. "Is this some kind of act?" she asked, leaning forward and peering into his face. "You're not some kind of professional party dancer, are you? Are you—" she wet her lips and glanced into his midnight eyes "—going to dress up like a genie and strip for me?" Hayley looked nervously around her backyard for the hidden cameras. "Because if you are, I don't go in for that kind of stuff...."

GT chuckled at her obvious mortification and pushed his foot off his knee. "No. I'm not a stripper. Or a dancer. I don't even know how to dance. At all. Honest," he said, leaning forward, elbows on knees, and taking her hand in his. "I'm your genie. You found my bottle on the beach today and released my powers."

Hayley snorted and, extracting her fingers from between his, patted his hand. "The only thing I released was a powerful foot odor." She drew her hand away. Physical contact with him played havoc with her reasoning abilities. Frowning, she rubbed her forehead and tried to think. How had he known about the bottle? Maybe he'd seen it in her beach bag? No, that was in the living room. Hmm. Must have been Mercedes again. Mercedes had known she would be sitting by their log at the beach and had planted the bottle. She grinned. Yeah, that Mercedes. What a nut.

"You wished for a cab, didn't you?"

"Well, I wished for a ride, so, uh, technically, yes, I did make a wish."

"And you wished for dinner, didn't you?"

Shrugging, Hayley returned his smile. "I hate to cook for just myself, so I always wish for dinner."

"Granted." GT slapped his thighs, then stood up and helped her to her feet. "Speaking of which, I need to get your salmon steaks on the grill and check that soufflé again."

How had he known that salmon was her favorite? Gracious, Mercedes had been thorough. "GT...or should I call you Genie?" Hayley asked, hurrying after him.

"GT's my name." He stopped in the doorway and winked at her with an intimacy that momentarily stalled her heart. "It stands for Genie, Third-class. But, since it's your birthday, you can call me anything your little heart desires. I answer to dear, darling, honey, stud muffin in a bottle, champion carpet driver.... I'm sure whatever you come up with will be fine,'' he called over his shoulder before making his way back to her oven.

Hayley rolled her eyes. "GT," she decided aloud, and reaching the kitchen, hopped back up on the stool. Grabbing a carrot stick from the relish tray, she toyed with it and debated whether or not she should let him know that she had guessed about the fact that someone—probably Mercedes—was throwing her a surprise party. Surely he must know that she'd figured it out by now. And if she was going to have guests, she'd appreciate a little warning.

"I don't suppose you could give me some idea of approximately when everyone is going to jump out of my closet?" She liked surprise parties, she just didn't like being, well, surprised.

"Hang on a second," he commanded, peeking into the oven. "Ah, perfect," he said, drawing the soufflé out and setting it on her chopping block. "Now, what's this about everyone jumping out of your closet?" He sent her a quizzical look.

"Okay." Hayley waved an impatient hand. "Out from under the bed, then. Who cares where, I would just like to know approximately when."

"Hey," GT shrugged. "Whatever you do on your own time is your own business. I'm just about wrapped up here, so I'll be taking off and getting out of your way."

He was leaving? Wasn't he going to stay for the inevitable party? No, Hayley thought, shaking her head in disappointment. He couldn't leave. Goodness, they hadn't even really had time to get acquainted yet. Quickly, she tried to think of ways to invite him to dally a little longer, without seeming . . . forward.

"What on earth am I supposed to do with all this food?" Her laugh was incredulous. There was enough here for several meals.

His brows arched innocently. "Eat it, I guess," he said with a light shrug.

"Oh, right. I live alone. I can't eat all this by myself."
She shot him a hopeful look. Maybe he would stay and help
her with it. "It seems like such a waste. I wish I had someone to share it with."

Tossing the salmon steaks on a platter, GT shook his
head. "Okay. Not my idea of a really great wish, but
hey—" his lips quirked at the corners "—whatever you
want."

Hayley's front doorbell chimed noisily.

GT held up the platter and inclined his head toward the
living room. "Could you get that? I'm just going to put
these babies on the grill."

Hayley scratched her temple in consternation as she made
her way to the front door. Who could it be? A tiny smile
hovered at her lips. Must be the group of friends and rela-
tives that Mercedes had assembled. Excited, she stopped at
the entry hall mirror and checked her hair and makeup
again. Still passable, she decided, and quickly practiced her
oh-gee-whiz-I'm-so-surprised expression.

Good. Okay. Taking a deep breath, she pulled open her
front door.

"Mercedes?" Drawing her lower lip between her teeth,
she cocked her head inquisitively. "What are you doing
here?" *And all alone,* she mused to herself. Hayley leaned
forward in the doorway and peeked around the corner for
Owen. Or perhaps a group of party guests, hiding in her
bushes. Finding no one, she pulled her friend inside her
house and threw the door shut. Everyone must be running
to the backyard. That was a good idea. Mercedes had
thought of everything. Then, as casually as she could, she
straightened her T-shirt and smoothed her shorts. It
wouldn't do to ruin Mercedes' fun by searching for the
party guests just yet.

"Hi," she said, smiling brightly, and patted her friend on
the arm.

"Hi, yourself," Mercedes replied, looking curiously at Hayley. The sound of GT's footsteps coming down the hallway toward the foyer drew her friend's interest.

"I'm not interrupting something here, am I?" Mercedes whispered, and patted her spiky hair as GT retrieved his leather jacket from the coatrack and tossed it over his shoulder. "Hubba-hubba," she murmured under her breath, "where'd you get *him?*" She quirked an appreciative brow in GT's direction.

Shaking her head, Hayley looked to the ceiling for help. "You should know," she said, her voice hushed as she elbowed her friend in the ribs. "You sent him. And," she cautioned at Mercedes puzzled expression, "you don't have to play dumb with me. Don't you think for a minute that I'm not on to you."

Striding toward the front door, GT stopped when he reached the two women. "Hi," he said, and nodded at Mercedes. "Hayley, the salmon steaks are on the grill. They will be done soon, so you'll want to go check them right away." Turning, he favored Mercedes with a lift of his finely chiseled lips. "Can't have all my hard work go up in smoke now, can we?"

"Oh, no-o..." Mercedes exhaled, her bug-eyed gaze trancelike.

Winking privately at Hayley with smoldering onyx eyes, he bent and kissed her lightly on the hand. "Happy birthday, Hayley. And ladies—" he pulled open the front door "—hope you enjoy your meal."

They both stood openmouthed and watched him saunter—in that casual, masculine way of his that had them both clutching each other for support—toward his waiting cab. Opening the door, he dropped inside and, with an automotive clap of thunder, was off.

"Wow," Mercedes murmured, her eyes round as the full moon. "Is he gorgeous, or *what?*"

"I guess he'd have to be, if he's an exotic dancer, right?" Hayley asked, her voice foreign and breathy in her own ears.

Mercedes gazed longingly after him. "Really? Wow."

Mercedes was good, Hayley thought, looking at her friend with admiration. *She* never would have been able to orchestrate such an amazing sequence of events, and act so convincingly innocent. Her heart swelled. She was so lucky to have such caring, creative friends. Throwing a companionable arm around her dearest chum, Hayley propelled her toward the kitchen. "I have to go out back," she said, and squeezed Mercedes' arm conspiratorially. "To...check the salmon."

"Terrific." Mercedes grinned happily. "It smells fabulous."

Speaking in a loud voice, for the benefit of the party that was most likely hiding in her backyard, Hayley entered the kitchen and asked brightly, "Gosh, Mercedes, what are you doing here tonight, anyway?"

Mercedes shrugged. "I don't know, I'm wondering the same thing. You're the one who called and insisted that I come help you eat the tons of food you suddenly found yourself in possession of." Her eyes darted around the kitchen, and she sniffed appreciatively. "This is definitely not like you."

"I called you?" Hayley shook her head. This must be part of the ruse, she thought, perplexed. Although, how dumb did they think she was? She hadn't called Mercedes. "I thought you had a date with Owen tonight."

"No—" Mercedes dug into the relish tray with relish "—that's next Friday."

Hayley raised a skeptical eyebrow, but decided to play along. "I must be losing it." She winked broadly. "Old age probably does that to you."

Mercedes laughed and trotted out to the backyard. "Well, come on, old lady," she called cheerfully over her shoulder, "let's eat. It smells heavenly out there."

Shivers of anticipation rapidly jumped one at a time down Hayley's vertebrae. She tried to arrange her face in a mask of ignorant bliss. But it was hard. Hopefully, GT would be out there, among the partygoers. And, hopefully, he would keep his clothes on. She wasn't ready for a birthday stripper. Taking a deep breath to calm her giddy nerves, she followed the sound of Mercedes' voice out back.

"Surprise!" Mercedes called, peeking under the grill. "The salmon is done already. We can eat."

Hayley stopped short and blinked. Where was everyone? She swallowed and glanced quickly around her yard. Not a party reveler in sight.

Grabbing the tongs, Mercedes lifted the salmon off the grill and arranged it on the platter that GT had so thoughtfully set out. "Yep," she proclaimed, turning to Hayley. "Done to perfection. Hmm. Looks like we're supposed to eat out here," she said, inspecting Hayley's patio table, set with all manner of culinary delicacies. "Come on, birthday girl," she urged, "sit down. You don't want it to get cold, now, do you?"

Confused, Hayley joined Mercedes at the table and watched dumbly as her friend loaded a plate of gourmet fare for each of them.

"So," Mercedes enthused, pouring them each a glass of wine from the funny-looking bottle GT had brought, "tell me all about this dreamy GT person." Taking a tentative sip of the wine, she nodded in approval, then dug into her meal.

"Well, since I saw you last," Hayley said between bites of GT's heavenly dinner, "Old Trusty died." Glancing surreptitiously at Mercedes, she searched for signs that her friend perhaps already knew about her car. Maybe even killed him herself as part of this harebrained plan.

"No kidding." Mercedes tsked in sympathy. "On your birthday? That's too bad."

"Yeah." Hayley blotted her lips with the linen napkin GT had set out. "Then, out of the blue, GT comes driving up and offers me a ride home in his cab."

Mercedes dangled her fork between her fingers. "Imagine that."

"Umm. Imagine that." Hayley grinned. "Then he drove me home. For free. When I got in the house, Mom was here. She told me that the cook had let her in. Then she left, and I found GT in my kitchen. Cooking this dinner."

Mercedes sat back and stared at her openmouthed. "Wow. You're kidding!" she marveled. "Is this some kind of birthday present from your mom?"

Cradling her wine goblet between her hands, Hayley regarded her friend with interest. Now, why would Mercedes ask that? Why wouldn't she want to take credit for this fantastic, creative and slightly insane plan? Unless... her mother was the one who'd arranged all this. *Mom?* Could Celeste have actually gone to all this trouble? Perhaps. Maybe she still felt bad about that surprise slumber party incident from Hayley's childhood and was trying to make up for it now.

Nah. Celeste's mind didn't work that way. This was more Mercedes' style.

"I don't know," Hayley answered, shrugging airily. "It doesn't really seem like something Mom would think of, but—" she smiled at Mercedes "—you never know."

"Speaking of mothers and their little quirks..." Mercedes groaned and began to regale Hayley with tales of Owen's mother.

They discussed what Owen had told her of the poor woman's obsessive-compulsive behavior for a while, and Mercedes' fears of meeting and eventually becoming daughter-in-law to this person. Then the topic turned to Technolabs, Inc., and the new general manager. From there it traveled to a new store at the mall, the good-looking guy at the coffee shop, and Mercedes' desire to try a new hair color. All the while, Hayley wondered when the party would begin.

"Well," Mercedes said, glancing at her watch after she'd polished off the last of her dessert. "I should probably be on my way."

"So soon?" Hayley asked, now completely bewildered. This was undoubtedly the weirdest party anyone had ever received. Although, she had to admit it had been fun. But she certainly wasn't ready for it to end. Not yet. The night was still young, she mused, even if she wasn't.

"Yes, hon," her friend answered, sighing. "I have a bunch of stuff I have to get done this weekend, and I need to get started on it tonight. But I'm so glad I could spend at least a few hours with you on your birthday. Too bad no one was around for a party." Mercedes stood. "Maybe next year, huh?"

Hayley looked suspiciously at the bushes in her side yard. "Yeah," she murmured hesitantly, "maybe next year."

"Have a happy birthday evening," Mercedes chirped, "and thanks for dinner. It was marvelous. My compliments to your chef." She smacked her lips in teasing appreciation. "Don't get up," she commanded. "I'll let myself out."

"Good . . . night," Hayley called and sat listening to the sounds of Mercedes getting into her car and driving off. What now? she wondered, suddenly feeling very lost and lonely, sitting there by herself in her backyard. She glanced at her watch. It wasn't even seven o'clock yet. Good heavens. There were endless hours till nightfall, it seemed.

Her doorbell chimed suddenly and she leapt to her feet, heart thundering fearsomely in the still summer evening. Was this finally it? she wondered as she threaded her way through her house toward the front door. Again, she paused at the entry hall mirror and inspected her reflection. She didn't look a year older, but if this unsurprise-type surprise party dragged out any longer, she was sure she'd begin to get gray hair.

Pulling open her front door, she found GT lounging casually against her door frame and smiling his sexy smile at her. Her heart crowded into her throat at the sight of him.

"*Now* do you believe me?" he asked, pushing off the doorjamb and grinning as he brushed past her into her house.

"Believe you?" she asked, poking her head out the door and glancing around.

"That I'm your genie?" Wandering into her living room, he dropped into her recliner and looked over to where she stood in the foyer.

Hayley shut the door and strode to her living room, pausing before the recliner and planting her hands firmly on her hips. "No."

"No?" he asked, tilting his head back and regarding her under the heavy hoods of his eyes. "Just like that? No?" He chuckled and, pushing against the chair, lifted the footrest and made himself at home.

Eyes narrowed, Hayley traced her lower lip with her tongue. "No. I don't think I do believe you. Where is the surprise party?" she demanded, becoming impatient at being toyed with. "Come on. I'm on to you guys."

He crossed his arms over his chest, seeming more amused than ever. "You're on to us, huh?" Shaking his head, he said, "Hayley, I hate to disappoint you, but there is no surprise party. It's just me. Your genie. Here to grant your wishes."

Hayley groaned and ambled over to her sofa, where she threw herself down and looked accusingly at him. He was far too attractive for her own good. Why on earth was he here, playing this game with her? Surely he must have fulfilled his agreement with Mercedes by now. He must have at least a dozen experienced, racy, worldly type women who would enjoy this farce. Why didn't he go play with them?

"Well, if you're my genie," she declared, pointing at him, "I've already wished three wishes. I wished for a ride home, I wished for the dinner and I wished for someone to share it with. You granted my three wishes, so what are you still doing here?"

GT laughed easily and closing his eyes, shook his dark head. "You've been watching too much *Aladdin* or 'I Dream of Jeannie.' You've got four more wishes. You get seven altogether. Didn't you read the instructions?"

Pursing her lips, Hayley sat up and stared at him. "What instructions?"

"The ones in the bottle. The bottle you found on the beach today."

"Oh. The *bottle*." She slapped her forehead dramatically with the palm of her hand. "Silly me. I didn't read the *instructions*," she said sarcastically, and reached for her beach bag that still sat at the end of her sofa. Celeste hadn't gotten around to throwing the bottle away before she left.

Removing the crusty, smelly old relic from her bag, she held it upside down over her coffee table and gave it a vigorous shake.

"Careful," GT instructed, pushing the footrest to her recliner down and striding across the room to where she sat. "I have to live in there from time to time."

"Oh," Hayley muttered skeptically, "poor you."

Taking the bottle from her hands, GT sat down next to her on the couch and peered into the neck of the place he called home. "Not here," he murmured, his thigh brushing lightly up against hers.

Hayley rubbed her damp palms on her shorts. He was sitting so close, she could feel the warmth radiate from his body. Did all genies smell this good, she wondered absently, then gave herself a mental kick. He was no genie. Just a cab-driving chef, hired to amuse her. She would do well to remember that, and not get too carried away with this fantasy. Although, she had to admit, the thought of having him as her own personal genie was appealing.

"What did you do with it?" he asked, dropping the bottle to the floor between his knees. He leaned closer still and looked at her.

"Uh...uh," she stammered. Her eyes darted to the two black diamonds that were his eyes. "With what?"

"The note," he said.

The note, the note, the note, she silently chanted in an effort to register whatever it was that he was talking about. He had such long, dark, incredibly thick lashes. Her eyes strayed to his mouth, where the beginning of a five o'clock shadow was beginning to form at his upper lip. Did genies shave? she wondered hazily. If she leaned just a little bit closer, she would be able to feel that stubble graze her own upper lip.

I wish he would kiss me, she mused dreamily, then, shocked at her train of thought, reared back from him, thankful that at least she hadn't spoken out loud. He'd probably been banking on her asking him to kiss her, knowing that he was irresistible to women. But no, she decided primly. She could resist him. Kissing was too easy. If he was going to actually attempt to grant her a wish, she'd make it a dilly.

"The note?" GT repeated, his eyes so piercing, Hayley was sure he could read her thoughts.

"Oh!" she exclaimed, remembering. "The *note!* That little scrap with all the stars and moons and the seven little squiggles?" She retrieved her purse and pulled out the aging piece of parchment with the funny markings. "Is this it?" she asked, handing it to him.

"Yep," he said, taking the small paper from her and smoothing it on his knee. He held it up for her inspection. "See? It says right here that you have four more wishes." He pressed the paper back into her hand.

"Where does it say that I have four more wishes?" she asked doubtfully, looking at him but pointing at the paper. "All I see are a bunch of squiggly little *L*s."

GT shook his head. "You're holding it upside down. Those are sevens. And," he continued as she righted the paper to its proper perspective, "as you can see, there are only four little sevens left." He pointed to the middle area. "That's because you've already made three wishes."

"Well, I'll be," Hayley murmured, studying the small page. He was right. But that didn't prove anything. Someone could have erased them. Maybe Mercedes had done it when she'd let herself out earlier.

"Listen," GT said, leaning dangerously toward her again, his words fanning her cheek, "you don't have to believe me yet. I understand. It's—" he paused, his eyes locking with hers "—hard to believe. So why don't you just make a wish? Just for fun."

His nose was a whisper away from touching hers, and, feeling a prickly blush steal into her cheeks, she ducked her head and pretended to study the note.

"I suppose," she squeaked, and, clearing her throat, shot her gaze back to his, "that you're hoping I'll uh, wish for . . . uh, you."

"No." He sighed, and Hayley saw a glimmer of something akin to disappointment flash across his handsome face. "I'm off-limits. Genie rule number 311. Anything else, though." He grinned invitingly. "Go ahead. If I'm right, your heart's desire will come true. If not, well, you can say 'I told you so,' I guess."

For some strange reason, as she sat looking at him, Hayley suddenly wished, with all her heart, that this cock-amamy story was for real. "Okay," she said, and drew a deep breath, "here goes."

Chapter Three

Even though her eyes were closed tightly in concentration, Hayley could feel GT watching her. He was probably afraid that she would wish for fame and fortune or some other such impossible nonsense, and he would have to admit that he was a fraud. No, she thought, as she nervously ran her tongue back and forth over her lower lip, she wouldn't waste time wishing for something so clichéd. Something that he could never grant. She would wish for something that just might be within the realm of possibility. She'd never wanted to be famous in the first place, and what good were riches if she didn't have anyone to share them with?

Burying her face in her hands, she racked her brain for something original. Inspiration struck as she remembered her conversation with Mercedes that afternoon.

Yes, she thought triumphantly, *that was it!* She would wish for a man. A partner in life. A man with one of the four shining qualities she found so appealing. After that, if her wish came true, she'd wish for a new and more interesting job.

But first, she'd go for the man. An adventurous guy that she could look forward to going out with while sitting at her computer every day. That would certainly perk up her days and make the job seem much less tedious. Too bad the guy seated next to her was off-limits.

What in heaven's name am I thinking? she wondered, slowly opening her eyes and squinting up at GT, who was still sitting only inches away. *He didn't have any kind of magical powers.* Why was she going along with this ludicrous game?

Because it's fun, a little voice in her head—the one that usually got her into trouble—shouted. And, because GT was one of the most exciting men she'd ever met. Sighing, she decided that even if this whole thing was just some big practical joke, she might as well throw herself into the moment and enjoy it for all it was worth.

"Ready?" GT's low voice caused her spine to melt.

"Yes."

"Okay. Go for it," he advised, looking expectantly at her. "Just be sure you phrase your request as a wish. I can't grant it otherwise. Genie rule number 214." Dimples deepened at the corners of his mouth as he grinned winsomely. "And, while I'm on the subject, from now until you use your seventh wish, if you say out loud that you wish for something, I have to grant it. Genie rule number 215. So—" he arched a teasing brow "—be careful what you wish, because you just might get what you ask for."

Hayley's breath caught in her throat. "Okay," she agreed, and following GT's instructions, carefully made her first wish. "I *wish* for an adventurous man."

Taken back, GT stared at her for a moment. "You mean, like MacGyver?"

Hayley grinned. "You get cable TV in that bottle?"

"I get around," he harrumphed defensively.

"I'll bet," she muttered under her breath. "No—not exactly like MacGyver. He doesn't have to be all that good-looking, really. I believe that it's what's inside that counts. Just give me someone who's adventurous and fun. Someone I can spend my free time with, and hopefully fall in love with someday. And . . . you know—" she lowered her eyes, feeling suddenly a little silly "—maybe have a couple of kids."

There, she thought smugly. If he wasn't a real genie, maybe he could still grant her wish. Maybe he had some adventurous-type friends he could fix her up with. Why waste time wishing for things that he would never be able to provide? Surely this was the most sensible way to approach his little charade.

"An adventurous man to have children with?"

"Umm, yes. Yes, that would be fine." Hayley smiled happily.

GT felt himself blanch. Sometimes he almost hated his job. The very idea of coming up with an adventurous man for Hayley to fall in love with and eventually father her children stuck in his craw. Feeling the need for air, he stood and dragged a hand through his hair. Why was he feeling so...jealous? He'd never had any problem granting a wish in the past. But, then again, Hayley had never been his client before, either.

"Okay." He sighed in disgust, knowing that he sounded like a petulant kid. Turning to face Hayley, he saw the expectant look on her face, and felt a wave of protectiveness toward this woman, so severe that it knocked the wind out of him more effectively than a punch in the gut. Taking a deep breath to steady his nerves, he rubbed his neck and hoped he was doing the right thing. "Granted," he said, somewhat churlishly.

The doorbell chimed.

Hayley's eyes widened in surprise. "Excuse me a moment," she said apologetically over her shoulder as she made her way to the door and pulled it open, only to find a bigger surprise than she'd ever imagined.

For there, standing on her front porch in a nylon jumpsuit, a helmet in his hands, was a diminutive man—probably no higher than Hayley's shoulder—in his late thirties. Several longish strands of his remaining hair had been combed artfully over his balding pate. And, whatever he may have lacked in stature, he made up for in beer belly.

"Are you ready to go?" the short, rotund dynamo demanded, obviously out of breath and in a fearsome hurry.

"Go?" Hayley asked, and glanced uneasily at GT, who'd come into the foyer and stood behind her. GT shrugged and grinned. "Go where?" she asked.

"To the airport," the curious-looking man barked impatiently. "Come on, doll face. We'd better hurry if we want to get several night jumps in." He glanced at his huge, expensive-looking gold watch, and then back up to Hayley. It was then he noticed GT. "Hi," he said, holding out his hand to the larger man with an assertion that took Hayley back. "Fred Peabody," he cried by way of introduction.

"I'm just the cable guy," GT said genially, grinning at Hayley's nonplussed expression.

"Oh." Fred dropped his hand and looked down his nose—as much as was possible—at the lowly cable guy. Grabbing Hayley by the hand, he yanked her out the door and halfway down the stairs before she knew what hit her. "Bust a move, doll face," he panted, hustling her rapidly to where his convertible waited, engine growling. Jerking open the door, he gestured for her to hop in.

"GT?" Hayley looked over her shoulder hesitantly.

"Have fun," GT called, and waved encouragingly. "Adventure awaits."

"*This* is the answer to my wish?" she managed to squeak as Fred stuffed her into his passenger seat and locked her in as though she were a child. While it was true she'd decided to lower her standards when it came to the men she dated, she couldn't help but wonder if Fred Peabody wasn't just a little too far out in left field.

"See you later!" GT called as Fred leapt over his door, faltering only when his filled-to-bursting nylon jumpsuit snagged on the lock. With a sharp nylon rip, he was free, and, adjusting a phone book beneath his generous behind, he threw the high performance engine into gear. Burning rubber noisily, he stomped on the gas and proceeded to tear down her street at a breakneck speed.

Hayley didn't have time to wonder how GT had accomplished this latest miracle. Although, whether it was her dream come true or not remained to be seen. Fred must have studied at the "Starsky and Hutch" school of driving, she decided nervously as he took a corner on two wheels, not bothering to stop for the red light.

"That's an SOB turn." He grinned wolfishly down at her where she lay sprawled across his lap.

Yes, she had to agree, the name fit not only the turn, but the driver, as well. "SOB?" she panted, struggling to right herself.

"Slide Over, Baby," he cried gleefully. With a death-defying screech of his brakes, Fred barely avoided colliding with a convoy of semitrucks as he merged onto the freeway and rocketed toward the airport.

Hair whipping painfully into her eyes, Hayley pounded the imaginary brake beneath her right foot and glanced over at Fred. His strands of long hair flew straight out behind him, revealing his balding head. Her heart thundered wildly in fear as she clutched the door handle and mentally cussed GT. This was his idea of *adventure?* Was he *crazy?*

Fred hunched over the wheel, in a seeming effort to create a better airfoil for what—if the mileage gauge could be believed—was warp speed. Taking his eyes off the road for a dangerously lengthy period of time, he leered over at her.

"Ever night-jump before?" he shouted, the wind tearing the words out of his mouth and flinging them behind him along with his hair.

"Night-jump?" Smoothing her own wildly whipping tresses back the best she could, she tried to look calm and interested. Remembering the vow she'd made to herself earlier that day, she decided to try to give Fred the benefit of the doubt.

"You know," Fred yelled, snaking a stubby arm around her shoulder and dragging her toward his phone book perch, "skydiving at—" he brought his fleshy lips to her ear and breathed heavily with meaning "—*night?*"

"*Skydiving?*" Hayley mouthed the word breathlessly as he zipped back and forth, changing lanes with the frequency of a jackrabbit on amphetamines. They were going skydiving? Oh, good heavens. She was terrified of heights. Almost as terrified as she was of Fred Peabody's driving skills.

"Yeah, skydiving in the dark. It's groovy," Fred crowed, obviously pleased with himself, the performance of his car and the babe he held captive at his armpit. "Beginners aren't supposed to be able to night-jump, but, if you don't tell, I won't." Fred wiggled his eyebrows meaningfully. "I heard you liked adventure. Great. Me, too."

"Where did you hear that?" she asked through her tightly clenched jaw, attempting to extricate herself from his possessive grasp.

"A mutual friend," he panted breathless. Ignoring the road completely, he nuzzled her ear, seemingly unaware of his date's need for space.

Mercedes, she thought murderously. She was going to kill Mercedes. This wasn't funny anymore. If she lived through this ride to the airport, she was going to give Mercedes a piece of her mind, she decided hysterically. What was left of her mind, that is. GT, too. He was on her list as well.

Along with her mother and anyone else connected with this crazy birthday gift.

Zooming along on a wing and a prayer, Fred sped past a large blinking sign at the side of the freeway that cautioned drivers to slow. Prepare to Stop, it flashed. Drawbridge in Motion. When Fred didn't appear to have any intention of stopping, Hayley's runaway heart bounced into her throat and she began to panic in earnest.

"Uh, Fred," she cautioned at the top of her lungs, tapping him on the arm to gain his attention. "Uh, Fred, the drawbridge is going up. You should probably slow down, like all these other people," she shouted above the wind and gestured to the cars that were obediently lining up to wait for the bridge to return to its original position. *"Fred!"* she screamed, pointing at the rising bridge as it loomed on the immediate horizon.

"Nah," Fred shouted, zooming onto the shoulder and aiming for the opening bridge, "it's not all the way up yet. We have plenty of time." Scooting forward on his phone book, he jammed the pedal to the metal, throwing Hayley back against her seat and freezing her screams of terror in her throat.

"These warnings," he shouted, pointing at the large sign that flashed *Stop...Stop...Stop...* "are for wimps. Hang on," he cautioned, ignoring the impassioned sign language of the bridge operator. He tossed an arm across her chest as the car careered up the ramp and suddenly became airborne.

Closing her eyes, Hayley let out a bloodcurdling scream that she was sure GT could hear clear back in the safety of her little house at Seventh and Elm.

The convertible touched down on the other side of the bridge, causing Hayley to suffer what was most likely a permanent case of whiplash. She couldn't open her eyes. Whether it was from the bone-jarring landing, or paralyzing fear, Hayley couldn't be certain, but she couldn't, and

wouldn't, open her eyes. However, she could tell by the
wind on her cheeks that they were still sailing toward the
airport. Covering her face with her hands, she prayed ear-
nestly for this hideous ride to end. But, for reasons she
would never fully understand, her prayers remained unan-
swered and she was tossed to and fro—for what seemed like
an eternity—like a leaf in a stiff breeze.

"Fred!" Hayley managed to shout, "I've decided that I
don't want to night-jump."

"Afraid?" he laughed. "Don't worry, doll face. You'll
love it. It's a rush."

Ignoring her protests, Fred whizzed through the parking
lot of the small airport, chased a taxiing private jet down
the runway and skidded to a stop next to a plane that sat
waiting to take off.

"Just in time," he panted, rushing Hayley out of his car
and into the waiting plane before she could object further.

Hustling a shell-shocked Hayley up to a bench seat near
the cockpit, Fred tossed her a nylon jumpsuit and helmet
similar to his own, before trotting to the tail of the plane to
check their parachute. Three other couples sat on the narrow benches that lined the plane's small cabin, chattering
excitedly among themselves.

Hayley stared out the plane's large sliding door into the
twilight. She was going to die on her birthday, she thought
morosely. Like some poetic character, she was going to fly
into the face of the sun—to her death. At the tender age of
twenty-seven.

Not.

No way in hell was she going to night-jump with Kami-
kaze Fred, she decided grimly. Throwing her jumpsuit and
helmet onto the floor, she stood and prepared to debark.

"Excuse me, excuse me," she said politely, making her
way past the three excitedly chattering couples toward the
door, "I just need to go..."

"So soon?" one of the jumpers joked. "We haven't even taken off yet." The small grouped laughed.

"All the better," Hayley responded, moving toward the door, only to have it slide shut in her face.

"Where do you think you're going?"

Hayley shut her eyes in frustration. If she had to use some of the more efficient moves she'd learned in her self-defense class on old Freddy boy, she would. Turning angrily, she clenched her fists and opened her eyes to discover an Adam's apple in her line of vision. Odd. Had Fred brought his phone book into the plane with them? Dragging her gaze upward, she gasped.

"GT!" She'd never been so happy to see anyone in her life. "What are you doing here?" she cried.

Pointing her toward the front of the plane, GT propelled her down the aisle to the cockpit. "Working," he said, stopping to snatch her jumpsuit off the floor. "Here. Put this on," he instructed. After settling into the pilot's seat, he donned his headset and began checking the instruments and starting the engines.

"You're the *pilot?*" Hayley gaped at him openmouthed. Would wonders never cease? He must have driven like a bat out of hell to get here as fast as Fred had. Or taken a magic carpet, she thought ironically, watching him prepare the plane for flight. GT was wearing a heavy, much-worn leather jacket with large buckles and silver snaps. There were some sort of military patches and badges of honor on the sleeves. One of these boasted the words God Help All of Us, Great London to Australia Air Derby of 1919.

Dragging her windblown hair away from her face and over her shoulder, Hayley watched GT at work. He seemed to know what he was doing, she thought with grudging admiration. It was very sexy, really, how he was just as at home in a kitchen as he was behind the controls of a plane. He seemed so natural, flipping switches and checking gauges. She only hoped he'd purchased the jacket at an antique store. It would be nice to know he'd flown more recently than 1919.

She shook her head. He hadn't even been born then, let alone flown a plane. She was losing it.

"Pacific tower, Beechcraft 240, Jim Dandy aircraft, taxi takeoff. Over." GT twisted around in his seat and looked up at Hayley. "You'd better get strapped in," he said, and turning back in his seat, listened for a moment then nodded. "We're cleared for taxi."

"But, but..." Hayley sputtered.

"Listen, Hayley, don't bug me," he interrupted impatiently. "I'm trying to concentrate. It's been a while since I've flown one of these babies and I need to think. Go sit down." When she didn't budge, he shouted above the roar of the propellers, *"Now!"*

The plane swung around as GT began to taxi them over to the runway. Hayley clutched the door to the cockpit for balance, and slowly and carefully made her way back to the bench, where she took her seat next to Fred.

"Here's the deal, doll face," Fred said, spittle flying as he attempted to be heard above the whine of the engines. "This is kind of a fancy, tag-team-type jump, capeesh? It's something our club has been experimenting with. Just watch, you'll get the hang of it."

"Tag team?" Hayley asked, glancing at the back of GT's head while Fred yabbered some nonsense in her ear. Over the din of her companion's babble, she heard GT say, "Pacific tower, Beechcraft 240 ready for takeoff."

Nodding to himself over something he'd apparently heard in his headset, he taxied onto the runway and paused. Hayley wondered if it was too late to escape.

"Beechcraft 240, Roger," GT responded again. And suddenly the plane began to pick up speed until they were moving rapidly down the runway.

It was too late, Hayley thought in horror, peering into the cockpit and watching GT pilot the aircraft. The tarmac fell away as he smoothly guided the plane into the eerie orange-and-blue star-filled sky above the earth.

Once they'd reached the proper altitude, the plane banked as GT headed for the night-jumping area. Fred prattled nonstop into Hayley's hair about heaven only knew what while she watched GT in fascination. Was there anything this guy couldn't do? Attempting to swallow back the sudden feelings of puppy love she felt growing over this larger-than-life hero, Hayley turned in her seat and tried to figure out what Fred was blathering about. That should kill any stray feelings of desire that were becoming weeds in her garden patch of sanity.

She couldn't afford to become all hung up on GT. He'd said he was off-limits, and she'd take him at his word. Obviously, he must have his reasons. Perhaps he was married. Her heart fell at the disturbing thought. Although, he didn't act married. And he wasn't wearing a ring.... But that didn't mean anything.

"And then I grab hold of your legs and hook your harness to mine, and then you pull the rip cord. Got that?" Fred demanded, thrusting a parachute into her hands.

What? What rip cord? Where? When? Hayley hadn't been listening, and Fred didn't seem to notice that she had absolutely no intention of leaving this plane. At least not as long as it was in the air.

"What?" Hayley shouted, and watched mortified as the first half of pair number one threw open the large sliding door and exited the aircraft, sans chute. *"Omigod!"* Hayley screamed, turning to stare in terror at GT. "He didn't have a parachute!"

"That's the whole idea, doll face," Fred crowed jubilantly.

The free-falling man's date, who was thankfully wearing their parachute, smiled and waved happily at the rest of the group before bounding headlong out of the plane and beginning to plummet at a horrifying speed toward her partner. Hayley only hoped that the woman was lucky enough to catch her daredevil date before it was too late. Not more than a minute passed before thrill-seeking couple number two repeated the performance.

Adrenaline began to pump furiously through her veins, thawing her from where she stood frozen, rooted to the middle of the aisle. This was insane. Eyes wild, Hayley began to back toward the cockpit. Deciding not to wait till they were on the ground to give GT a piece of her mind, she joined him where he sat piloting the plane and smacked him rudely with the parachute that Fred had given her.

"Is this your idea of a *date with an adventurous man?*" she demanded, gesturing frantically to where Fred and the remaining couple stood preparing to jump. "I could get myself killed out there!" she cried, tears of hysteria welling into her eyes as she tightly clutched her chute.

"Hey," GT said with a shrug, putting the plane on autopilot, "you said you wanted adventure, and—" he grinned sheepishly at her "—now you have it."

It had seemed like such a good idea at the time, he thought, beginning to reevaluate his plan. After all, it had been exactly what she'd ordered. Hadn't she said that looks weren't important, and that adventure was? His conscience began to work overtime as he realized he'd been wrong. What had gotten into him?

Usually, the clients were thrilled with the results of a job, but this time, he had the feeling that he'd let his heart rule his head. He'd given her a man she couldn't possibly fall for.

Bad mistake.

Passing a hand over his face, he looked guiltily up at her. He didn't blame her for being unhappy with Fred. Under similar circumstances, he'd be pretty ticked off, too. Plus, she had a point about the danger involved. It wouldn't do to jeopardize a client. Especially not a client he liked as much as he liked Hayley.

As tears clung to her lashes, he felt something give in his soul, and knew he had to make a few changes in this wish. It rarely ever happened, but this time he'd make an exception. After all, he was partly to blame.

Hayley whapped him with her chute again. "I never asked for *this!*" she shouted, glancing back over her shoulder just in time to catch the second-to-last couple exiting the plane.

"Come on, doll face," Fred yelled, anxious to be on his way. "It's our turn."

Hayley looked firmly at GT. "I'm just going to go tell him that we're not going tonight. No way am I jumping out of this plane. I don't care if it ruins everyone's fun. Tough," she spat, indignation overriding her fear. Turning on her heel she marched down the aisle toward Fred.

Taking her approach as the signal to go, Fred saluted jauntily before flinging himself out the door.

"Omigod! GT! Omigod!" Hayley jumped up and down in horror, then, running to the door, peered out into the darkness, searching for Fred. *"GT!* He doesn't have his chute!" she screamed, holding their chute up as evidence. "I have to go get him," she panted, hysteria rising as she struggled to figure out the straps of her parachute.

GT strode out of the cockpit, the plane on autopilot and flying smoothly in the calm evening air. "Oh, no, you don't," he said, grabbing her around the waist and hauling her away from the door. "I've changed my mind. You're not ready for skydiving yet." Disentangling the straps from her fingers, he tossed the chute to the floor.

"B-b-but, what about poor Fred?" she stammered, sobbing in GT's arms. "He's going to be killed." She felt no great love for the devil-may-care dwarf, but she didn't wish him dead. And even Fred with his nine lives couldn't survive a free-fall from a plane without a parachute.

"Don't worry," GT assured her, and kicked the chute out the door. "He'll be fine."

Chapter Four

The wind whipped Hayley's hair into her face as they soared down the freeway, leaving the airport behind. But this time she wasn't afraid. No, this time her arms were locked firmly around GT's waist as she leaned her cheek against his leather-clad back and enjoyed the experience. She'd never known riding a motorcycle could be so much fun.

Maybe she was able to let go and relax because GT seemed as competent on a motorcycle as he was in a plane. Or maybe it was because her date with Fred Peabody was officially over. Whatever the reason, she was having the time of her life speeding toward a restaurant that GT had recommended.

Amazingly enough, Fred had managed to catch his parachute, put it on and make it safely to the ground without so much as a stubbed toe. Much to Hayley's disbelief, the strange man had been inordinately pleased with the way the new and improved stunt had worked out, and wondered if she'd be up for trying it again some day. It was his suggestion that she could stay in the plane, throw him the chute and then take pictures. Hayley had thanked him for his interest, but let him know in no uncertain terms that he should look elsewhere for a partner in adventure.

Mentally, Hayley scratched adventurous off the list of qualities she found appealing in a man, and substituted boring. Leaning with GT as he guided the bike around a curve in the road, Hayley decided that if she was ever going to spend much time with an adventurous man, he would have to be a lot like GT. Certainly GT was not boring, but at least he was sane.

And handsome. Perhaps she should stop telling everyone that looks didn't matter, she thought, inhaling deeply and relishing the scent of leather. Because if she was honest with herself, they did. Just a little. After all, poor Fred didn't stand a chance in her mind's eye when she compared him to GT.

Hayley could feel her stomach rumble along with the bike's engine, and suddenly realized she was ravenous. She hadn't eaten very much of GT's gourmet dinner. She'd been too uptight about getting caught with her mouth full by her surprise party guests.

Thankfully, flying made him hungry, GT had told her. He'd also claimed he wanted to make up for the adventurous blind date fiasco by taking her out for a midnight dinner. She'd agreed, finally coming to terms with the fact that she probably wasn't going to get a regular surprise party. No, she decided, her heart pounding with exhilaration, there had been nothing regular about today. She smiled against the warm leather at his broad back and watched the city lights flash by as GT wove through the side streets to a part of town she was not familiar with.

Tightening her arms around his waist, she felt a shudder of excitement surge into her throat. Her birthday was nearly over, and she could think of no one she'd rather spend the last few hours with than her supposed genie.

She still wasn't a believer in his cock-and-bull genie story, but she had to give him credit. He was good. At everything, it seemed. Where on earth had Mercedes found him? He called her his client, so he must work for some kind of party business or escort service. Lord knew he was good-looking enough.

Pulling the motorcycle to a stop in front of a big brick building in a desolate, industrial-looking section of town, GT dismounted and helped Hayley to her feet. "This is it." He pointed to the dark entrance.

"This is a restaurant?" Hayley asked, staring at the imposing brick building that looked for all the world like a deserted warehouse.

"Yep. This is Sultan's." He grinned engagingly at her under the dim light of the street lamp. "It's one of my favorites."

"I've never noticed this place before," she murmured as GT slipped his hand into hers and led her to the large, ornate double doors. As a matter of fact, she thought confused, she'd never noticed this entire section of town before. But then, she didn't have much call to wander unescorted into the industrial areas. Especially at night.

Pausing before opening the door for her, GT held her hand up and lightly kissed her fingertips. "I hope you like eating with these," he whispered. She could feel his warm lips moving against the sensitive pads of her fingers as he spoke. Giddy butterflies took wing in her stomach. "They don't use silverware in this place."

She didn't care. She would eat with *his* fingers if it meant spending a few more glorious hours in his presence. With a slight, clearing shake of her head, she wondered what had happened to her fury toward him over her date with Fred "Adventureman" Peabody. Only a few hours ago, she'd been raging. And now she was as ebullient as a schoolgirl. GT had a way of doing strange things to her emotions. She would have to watch herself around him.

As they headed inside, Hayley decided that Sultan's was aptly named. For, beyond the intricately carved doors lay a study in what she imagined an ancient Muslim ruler's tent to look like. Tapestries hung in great billows from the ceiling, turning the light into a dim, pinkish glow. The walls were covered with Turkish rugs and baskets and brightly colored gold-gilded ornaments and exotic-looking bric-a-brac. But most interesting to Hayley was the fact that the tables all sat low on the floor, surrounded by leather bean-bag-type cushions.

"Come on," GT whispered, pulling her to a table in a dark back corner. "Let's sit by ourselves, away from the crowd."

"Okay," she murmured, trailing behind him, her hand in his. Spending a quiet evening getting to know GT sounded immensely desirable.

Once they were settled comfortably on their respective beanbags, Hayley leaned on her elbows and looked across the low table at GT. "So, do you come here often?" she asked, curious about the other women he brought here.

"I used to. A long time ago, when I was younger. But not recently."

"Why not?"

"Work keeps me busy."

"Work?" Hayley grinned. "You mean being a professional genie."

Appealing dimples came out of hiding. "It's harder than it looks."

"You make it look easy."

GT winked lazily at her. "Practice."

"So, you have to know how to fly a plane to be a genie? And cook? And... drive a cab?"

"It helps." He shrugged loosely.

"What else can you do?" she quizzed in an effort to gain clues to his real line of work.

GT's mouth quirked in amusement. "Oh, this and that."

"This and that?" Hayley laughed. "And I suppose you can do this and that pretty well, too."

"Some things better than others." He grinned his sexy grin and winked lazily at her again.

Lowering her eyes, Hayley was grateful that the room was dim enough to hide her red-hot cheeks. She'd set herself up for that one. The double meaning to his innocent words had a remarkable effect on her blood pressure. Luckily, their server finally arrived, sporting a turban, blousy pantaloons and shirt cinched tightly at the waist with a bright sash. He carried a large silver bowl and a silver pot with a long spout.

"Abba abba dabba?" he asked happily, and looked with great admiration at Hayley.

"I, uh, yes. Sure." Hayley shrugged, feeling too self-conscious to ask the poor man to repeat himself. Some tea from that big pot would probably hit the spot. After a moment had passed and the waiter just stood there, ogling her, she looked over at GT for help.

GT inclined his head toward the bowl. "He wants to wash your hands."

"Wash my hands?" Hayley's face scrunched in consternation. "Why?" The way the young man was standing there, undressing her with his eyes, Hayley had the feeling he was hoping she'd strip down to her skivvies and take a bath right there in the middle of the restaurant.

"Because you're going to be eating with them. It's a courtesy. Here—" he demonstrated by putting his hands in the bowl "—like this."

"Oh." Hayley followed suit and smiled up at the waiter as he poured water from his silver pot over her hands and fingers, and jabbered ninety miles an hour to her in an accent that only distantly resembled English. "Ha, ha, yes," she answered, laughing politely at some witty remark he'd made that she didn't understand. He seemed immensely pleased.

Speaking rapidly in the waiter's own tongue, GT shook his head at the man and gestured possessively at Hayley. Looking disappointed, the waiter suddenly seemed to bow under the weight of his turban and, taking his bowl and pot, moved over to a sideboard that was loaded with towels.

"What was that all about?" Hayley whispered, and wondered what to do with her dripping hands.

GT grinned. "He just told you that he's in love with you and wonders if you would be interested in giving him some sons."

"Me?" Hayley squeaked.

"Mmm," GT nodded, arching an eyebrow. "He was very pleased when you laughed and said yes."

Her eyes widened. *"He was?"*

"Don't worry," GT whispered, "I told him you were mine."

"You did?" Hayley's heart lurched into her throat as GT's eyes pulled her into their black vortex. Her voice was thready in her ears. "Oh, well, uh, thank you. I guess. Did he, um, you know, buy that?" she whispered as the waiter approached.

"He seemed to," GT whispered back, his eyes twinkling. "But he said that if I ever grew tired of you, to let him know. He would treat you like a princess."

Hayley touched her tongue to her lower lip. "What did you tell him?"

GT took a deep breath, his expression becoming unreadable. "I told him that he would have to go through me to get to you. And that there was little likelihood that I would ever grow tired of you."

"Oh." Her eyes met his in a supercharged moment that left her head spinning. Unable to sustain his gaze, she tore her eyes away and glanced up as the waiter, who made no effort to hide the yearning in his expression, arrived. For lack of something better to do she stared fascinated at her still dripping hands.

The young man was adorable, really. But compared to GT, he was just a kid. Handing them each a white towel, the waiter fawned over Hayley and instructed, "Dabba." He held her hand a moment longer than was necessary as he retrieved her towel, and then, noticing GT's scowl, passed out the menus and quickly disappeared.

"You can actually understand what he's saying?" Hayley asked, looking incredulously at GT as though it were the most remarkable feat he'd performed to date. "I suppose speaking foreign languages is just another aspect of your job description?"

GT's nod was offhand. "Our waiter is from the same country where my work is headquartered." Shrugging lightly, he tossed his menu on the table. "And I have to travel a lot for my job, so speaking several languages can come in handy."

"What's the name of this mysterious company you work for? Rent-a-Genie?" she quipped, tongue in cheek.

"Something like that," he responded dryly.

"That must be interesting," she commented in an effort to make small talk as she scanned the menu for some kind of food that she recognized.

"Sometimes more than other times." He smiled meaningfully at her. The waiter returned, and with some lightning-fast verbiage aimed at GT, took their order and gathered their menus. Shaking his head, GT answered the waiter's parting questions, then waved him away.

"I'm afraid to ask," Hayley said, glancing at their server's retreating back as he shuffled slowly off.

"He wondered if I'd changed my mind."

"Oh."

"I told him no."

"Oh."

Ducking her head shyly, Hayley attempted to steer the conversation to safer ground. "So. You're not from around here?"

Laughing, GT leaned back in his cushion and studied her through the relaxed slits of his eyes. He shook his head in mock sadness. "You still don't believe, do you?"

"Convince me," she challenged boldly.

GT liked her. He hadn't known her for more than half a day, but already he was completely and totally captivated by her. Out of the hundreds of people he'd worked for and had the pleasure of doing business with, she was by far the spunkiest, most compassionate, and altogether sexiest woman he'd ever met.

It was too bad that he couldn't act on these feelings, he thought grumpily, and rubbed his neck in an effort to ease the tension he felt building. But no. Rule 311 was not meant to be taken lightly. Those who broke this cardinal rule suffered grim consequences for their choice. Giving his head a slight shake, he made a conscious effort to clear his mind. It didn't bear thinking about. Besides, he could never have a relationship with Hayley. He was too set in his ways.

"You mean to tell me that I haven't convinced you yet?" Sitting up straighter in his seat, he leaned toward her. "I granted four out of seven wishes. Doesn't that prove anything?" He feigned hurt feelings.

"No. That was all just part of the birthday trick that Mercedes hired you to play. And the rest of it is a coincidence," she said, passing his feats of derring-do off easily.

GT's upper lip curled in amusement. "I'd like to see you pull off some of those tricks without a little genie power."

"I could do it," she replied, staunchly defending her position. "I'd just need a little help and some time to plan."

"I see." GT grinned affably.

The waiter returned with the appetizer. Setting a plate of what looked like green salsa on the table, he held out a basket of bread. "Abba dabba abba abba dab dab." He jabbered on and motioned to the green slush, then, wiggling his eyebrows at Hayley, darted away.

GT translated. "Dip the bread into the vegetables."

"Oh, sure." Hayley dubiously eyed the concoction. "I think he said 'I have cleaned out the disposal for your dining pleasure.'" Hayley dipped her bread and tasted it. "Mmm. Good, though," she praised, and continued to eat with gusto.

"Hmm. Your interpretation is actually pretty close," he said in mock seriousness. "What he really said was that he'd cleaned out the lawn mower's clipping catcher."

"Fine—" Hayley giggled "—as long as he didn't say he'd cleaned out the stall."

They laughed and joked and played with their food till the other patrons in the restaurant were looking over at their private corner with amusement. The fare was excellent, and once Hayley got the hang of eating everything from the appetizer to the main course to the crusty pastry dessert with her fingers, she decided that the habit may be worth adopting at home. It was liberating.

For some reason, it took away the stiff, formal feelings of discomfort normally associated with a first date. Not that this was a first date, of course, she amended to herself. Nevertheless, she found herself to be curiously comfortable with GT. As comfortable as she could be given the horrific crush she was beginning to develop on him. She knew it was idiotic, but couldn't seem to help herself.

Between the whispered giggles, the finger food and her infatuation with GT, Hayley felt as if she were suddenly transported back to her youth. The buoyant feelings were wonderful, considering that as of today she was officially another year older, with nothing interesting in her foreseeable future.

In an effort to cast off the dismal image that flitted through her mind of herself one day receiving the senior citizen discount at the Technolabs cafeteria, Hayley looked at GT and grinned. "So. Fred Peabody is your idea of my heart's desire," she stated, and watched him duck his head remorsefully. "If that's the case, I'm not so sure I want to take you up on my last three wishes."

"Okay, okay. So I had an off day." He swung his gaze to collide with hers. "Give me another chance. I promise, I'll make it up to you. Besides," he said, looking at her beseechingly, "if I don't grant all seven of your wishes, I can't go home. Genie rule number 77."

"You can't go home?" Hayley frowned, trying valiantly to ignore his boyish charm. "Then where will you stay?" If he had to grant her three more wishes, he would be around at least until tomorrow. Unless Mercedes had only hired him for the day. If that were the case, she had the sneaking suspicion that after her birthday was officially over, she'd never see him again. The thought depressed her.

"I'll just take my bottle and stay in my cab. That is, if you don't mind if I park it in your driveway."

Hayley snorted. He was taking the genie routine just a little too far. His bottle. That was a laugh. Just how gullible did he think she was? No one in their right mind could believe that he actually lived in that corroded old bottle. Deciding to ignore the ridiculous reference, she asked, "Your cab? That can't be very comfortable."

A slow smile crinkled at the corners of his eyes. "You'd be surprised."

Hayley cringed as an ugly thought occurred to her. Could his wife have thrown him out of the house? Is that why he didn't have anywhere to go? As much as she hated the idea that he wasn't single, she hated the idea of developing a crush on a married man even more. Never one to stand on ceremony, Hayley decided that the sooner she found out the dreaded truth, the better.

"Are you married?" she asked, looking suspiciously at him.

Laughing good-naturedly, GT shook his head. "No. Why?"

"Well," she said, feeling suddenly foolish, "uh, a jack-of-all-trades, such as yourself, uh, has probably turned a few heads..." Her voice trailed off lamely.

"I guess I've been tempted to take the matrimonial plunge in my time, yes." His coal black eyes grew reflective as he spoke. "But, in my line of work, it wouldn't be fair to anyone. My job is so demanding that I'd almost never be home. I have to travel most of the year, and I know from experience that long-distance relationships rarely work out." He smiled ruefully. "On the odd occasion that I am back home for any length of time, I visit with family and friends for a few days before being reassigned to a new client. Doesn't leave much time to get serious with anyone from my neck of the woods."

Experiencing a curious mix of emotions, Hayley knew that on one hand she was thrilled to discover that GT wasn't married. But, on the other hand, she was disappointed that his job kept him away from home so much of the time. He was right. Whatever his line of work really was, it sounded like it would never be conducive to a happy marriage.

"And you can't date your clients?" She was horrified to hear herself blurt the words out. For pity's sake. Why couldn't she just take the hint? He'd told her he was off-limits. Perhaps that's what she found so alluring about him. The old adage about people wanting what they couldn't have was certainly true in this case.

In any event, she had to get a grip. She barely knew this guy, yet she was acting like a teenage groupie. Must be the pilot thing. Or maybe the motorcycle thing. Or maybe it was his dark, incredibly sexy bedroom eyes... She wriggled around in her seat in an attempt to shake off the spell she'd obviously fallen victim to. "I'm sorry," she amended, trying to appear blasé. Backpedaling, she added, "It's really none of my business."

Sighing, GT leaned forward and looked thoughtfully at her for a moment. "No. It's all right." His voice held a note of melancholy. Passing a frustrated hand over his jaw he searched her face, seemingly deep in thought. "It's not that we can't date the client, exactly," he began slowly. "It's what the dating leads to that causes the problem."

Drawing her lower lip into her mouth, Hayley nodded in understanding. "Oh, well, of course. I've heard of that. Lots of companies have rules against internal fraternizing."

"No," he said, "you don't understand."

Hayley looked blankly at him, not wanting to pry, but insatiably curious about his love life. "That's okay." She smiled brightly and hoped she sounded offhand. "Like I said, it's none of my business. You don't have to tell me."

"No. I want to. It's just that..." Taking a deep breath, GT appeared to make a decision. "In my line of work, falling in love with a client means losing my immortality."

"Losing your...immortality?" Hayley shook her head. He was right. She didn't understand. Was this some kind of code word for an employee benefits package? Hadn't Mercedes mentioned another in the endless barrage of Technolabs memos about some kind of life insurance policy called Immortality Life?

"Yes. I know you're going to find this as hard to believe as the fact that I'm a genie, but—" he glanced up at her, his eyes begging her to try to understand "—if a genie falls in love with a mortal woman, he loses his immortality." His heart constricted painfully at the look of confusion on Hayley's face. She was reading something into his words that wasn't there. She was taking it personally. Sighing, GT plowed a weary hand through his hair. This was another one of those little things he hated about his job. Explaining the whole immortality premise to a skeptic. Telling the client that he couldn't get involved in their personal life. It rarely ever came up, but he should have figured that with

Hayley, it would eventually be an issue. Because if ever there was a woman he'd consider giving up his immortality for, Hayley was it.

Leaning forward, GT took Hayley's delicate hand in his. How could he make her understand that he was a company man? He loved his job. Falling in love with a mortal woman was out of the question. "I don't make up the rules. I just follow them. I've personally known only one genie who traded it all in for the love of a mortal woman. He quit the company and ran off to live out what was left of his life with her."

Hayley arched a curious brow. "So, what's wrong with that? It sounds romantic."

"Well, death, for starters." Smiling ruefully, GT released her hand and shrugged. "It's not my bag."

"We all have to die sometime."

"That's the beauty of being a genie." GT's eyes pierced hers. "We don't."

"You never have to die?" Hayley asked, incredulous. Funny, she thought, taking in the grim set of his jaw. When he was so serious like this, she could almost believe him.

"Never."

"So you go through eternity, never experiencing true love?" she asked skeptically. How could that be? It sounded dreadful to her. Hayley couldn't imagine giving up her dreams of a man and babies to call her own for her employer. Especially not Technolabs. She would much sooner spend her life, short as her time was here on this earth, knowing the feel of a child's chubby cheek against her own, or the comforting strength of a loving man's embrace. To live forever without these simple pleasures was her idea of hell.

"There are other things in life," GT said gently, defending his decision.

Hayley arched a brow. "You're right. I don't believe you. But if I did . . . and if I had to choose, I'd choose love."

GT shook his head, unable to understand. "Love over life?"

"Sure. That's why I wished for an adventurous man. I wanted somebody exciting to share my life with. To grow old with. Eventually, to die with." She waggled a teasing finger at him. "I just don't happen to want the somebody exciting that you provided. I have a feeling the dying part would come a little prematurely with a nut like Fred." Laying her cheek in her hand, she tilted her head and smiled. "The way I see it, I'm going to eventually get both. What good is life without love, anyway?"

"Sometimes it's pretty damn good." He winked lazily at her.

"I feel sorry for you."

"Don't. I don't have it so bad."

Well, she thought, if he's happy without the love of a good woman, then more power to him. It wasn't her job to teach an old leopard new spots, or whatever that other old adage was.

"True." Hayley grinned brightly, as she attempted to shake off the depressing tone of their conversation. "You don't have it so bad. And it's not like we're in any danger of falling in love."

"No."

Hayley couldn't be sure, exactly, but she almost fancied that a look of disappointment briefly flashed across GT's face. No, she decided, mentally chiding herself over this ridiculous schoolgirl crush. It was probably just wishful thinking.

"Here you go," Hayley said, retrieving GT's supposed apartment-bottle from where he'd left it on the floor in front of her couch. She handed him the barnacle-encrusted relic and turned to face him in the dim glow of her living room lamp. Shivering slightly—whether from the early morning chill or from the close proximity of the man be-

fore her, she couldn't be sure—she wrapped her arms
around her middle and tried to smile past the feelings of
post-party depression. "Would you like an extra blanket?" she asked, still wondering why a guy like him would
spend the night in that broken-down excuse for a taxi.
Surely Mercedes had paid him enough money to afford a
nice hotel room somewhere. Heavens, with all the jobs he'd
had to do today, Mercedes would have to work overtime for
a year.

GT shook his head. "No, I'll be fine," he assured her,
and began to walk slowly through the hallway toward her
front door.

"You're sure?" She followed him out the door to her
stoop. The air seemed cool for July, she noted, briskly
rubbing her forearms for warmth. The porch was dark except for the moon's luminescence. "Because I wouldn't
mind if you wanted to, you know, crash on my couch or
something...."

"Hayley," he chided gently. "I said I'll be fine."

"Okay." She tried to keep the note of doubt out of her
voice. She knew he had a thing about staying away from his
clients, but this was ridiculous. Oh, well, if he wanted to
continue the charade, far be it from her to stop him.

"You should put a sweater on, though. You look a little
chilly."

"I'm fine," she said, playing his game.

"Well, good night," he said, stepping off the top step
and turning toward her. Starlight shimmered in his eyes.

"Good night," she whispered, wondering if he would
still be around in the morning. "Thank you for a wonderful birthday." In spite of everything, she'd had a fabulous
time. Because of GT, it was a birthday she wouldn't soon
forget.

"My pleasure," he said, reaching out and hooking her
little finger with his. "How old are you now, anyway?" he
asked, swinging their hands loosely back and forth.

Hayley batted his arm with her free hand in mock offense. "Don't you know it's impolite to ask a lady her age?"

"Ah—" he shrugged playfully "—well, that would explain why I'm still single."

"Most likely." She nodded solemnly. "I'm twenty-seven."

"Twenty-seven? On the seventh day of the seventh month? Hmm." GT mused thoughtfully as he reached up and traced her brass house numbers on the porch post— 777—with the back of his forefinger. "Something almost magical about that, wouldn't you agree?"

"Definitely," Hayley murmured, mesmerized by the sultry pull of his voice.

Tugging on her fingers, GT drew her to the edge of her stoop. From where he stood on the step below her, he was able to look directly into her eyes. No jewels in any sheikh's treasure trove could ever compare to the sapphire beauty he found there. There was something different about this woman. Something that defied description. He would have to be careful around her, he reminded himself as he propelled her slowly into his embrace. Keep her at arm's length. Not allow himself to get too close. Remember that he had a job to do, and to keep useless emotions at bay. A feeling of restlessness consumed him as he stood absorbing her essence.

"Happy birthday," he whispered above the roar of his hammering pulse. He felt her arms loosely encircle his waist, and giving into a primal, nearly uncontrollable need, he buried his face in the silky waves of her hair.

This lack of professional objectivity was vaguely disturbing to him, although not enough to really worry about. Not yet, anyway. Certainly there could be no harm in a friendly birthday kiss, he thought, lifting his face away from her fragrant tresses and tilting her chin up with the tips of his fingers.

"Thank you," she whispered back, through the shadows, her lips mere inches from his own. "And, thank you for saving my life, too," she added, her eyes flashing.

"Anytime," he said before he lowered his mouth to hers. He only hoped that, when the time came, she'd return the favor.

Chapter Five

As GT's mouth moved gently over hers, Hayley felt her knees grow weak with yearning. It was so unfair, she thought dizzily, lost in the hypnotic pull of his touch. Deep in her soul, she knew that this was the man she'd been waiting for all her life, and unfortunately, she couldn't have him. Hovering at the edge of the porch, she arched toward him and ran her hands up over his broad back, reveling in the feel of muscle and soft, well-worn leather.

He gripped her arms, pulling her against the hard wall of his chest, and then buried his hands in her hair. Angling her mouth more firmly beneath his, the gentle good-night kiss quickly flared into something quite different. Her heart leapt and her breathing became ragged as he kissed her with a smoldering possession that stunned her. What happened to his stout rules against client involvement? Surely he didn't kiss all his clients this way, she thought, as an involuntary moan surged into her throat.

She gasped for air as GT momentarily tore his lips from hers, then, seeming to lose an internal battle, captured her mouth for more. Hayley had never felt such exquisite sensations as her insides turned to liquid and surged hotly through her body. Boldly tasting him back, she matched his desire, kiss for kiss. Pulses singing, her hands took on a life of their own, exploring his soft midnight hair, his broad shoulders, the bulge of his bicep and the square lines of his jaw.

Too intoxicated to wonder why she felt so perfectly natural, standing there on her front porch, passionately kissing a man who she'd only just met—a man who not only made the crazy claim to be her genie, but who had made it perfectly clear that he had no intention of ever allowing himself to fall in love—Hayley gave herself up to the moment.

After all, it was her birthday. And she deserved a little excitement. She was certain that from this day forward, no matter how boring her job at Technolabs might be, she could always just close her eyes to the drudgery and dream of GT.

GT circled his arms firmly at her waist, then lifted her off the porch and let her slide down the firm planes of his body to stand on the top step with him. He dragged his lips away from hers and laid his forehead against her brow.

"Hayley," he whispered, his voice hoarse, his breathing still quick. "I can't do this."

Disappointed, Hayley nodded mutely. Of course. Good old excuse number 311. Thou shalt not kiss the client. "I know," she said, pulling back against his embrace and looking off over his shoulder. She was too mortified to look him in the eye. "I'm sorry. I didn't mean to get you into trouble or anything...." Her voice trailed off miserably.

"Hey, it's not your fault. It's mine. Honest," he pulled her back against his chest and cradled her head against the steady beat of his heart. "I'm the one who started it. And I should know better. I'm the one who should apologize."

Apologize? she wondered dully. *For what?* For giving her the most thrilling day of her life? For kissing her like she'd never been kissed before? Or maybe he was just plain sorry for lonely little Hayley. The poor girl who had no one to celebrate her birthday with. The pathetic creature who was so hard up for companionship, she practically threw herself at him, even when he'd made it perfectly clear that he had no interest in her. At least no romantic interest.

Well, she didn't need his pity. She may be another year older and without a man in her life, but that didn't make her some kind of charity case, she thought, bristling.

"No need to apologize," she informed him, taking a step back and smiling as nonchalantly as she could muster, given the fact that her knees had suddenly turned to pudding. "I wouldn't want to mess with your, er, mortality," she said lightly, trying to keep the hurt and sarcasm from her voice.

Concern filled his eyes as he looked at her for a long moment, then dropped his hands from where they'd been gripping her arms.

Anxious to smooth over the awkward situation, Hayley quickly crossed the porch and, turning at her front door, paused and pushed her lips into a pseudo smile.

"I hope we can still be friends," she said for lack of a better cliché, and stepped into her front hall.

"No harm done," he assured her just before she closed her door and shot the bolt.

Hayley woke to the sounds of the neighbor's dog giving the paperboy a run for his money mingling with the steady purr of Old Trusty's engine, as they filtered to her through the bedroom window. *Old Trusty was purring?* she thought muzzily, rubbing her eyes and stretching. She sat up in bed and smoothed her tangled mass of hair away from her face. How could that be? Old Trusty was not only still at the beach, he was dead.

Throwing back the covers she sat on the edge of the bed and sniffed the air. Coffee? Her pulse accelerated. GT? She scooted off the bed and ran to the window. *GT!* Her throat constricted joyfully. Sure enough, there he was, standing on the lawn near her driveway, wearing nothing but a pair of faded blue jeans and a contented smile, as he stood watching some mechanical mystery unfold beneath the hood of her car. Hayley pulled her lower lip into her mouth and stared.

Wow. He had a beautiful build. Not like the cover of *Muscleman Monthly* by any means, but strong and powerful and sinewy and tan and, well, as far as she was concerned, pretty much perfect. His longish black hair glittered in the sunlight, and he pushed it back out of his face and ran a hand over the dark stubble at his jaw. Taking a sip from his coffee cup, he turned slightly and glanced back at the house, as though he felt her gaze on him. Catching her eye as she watched him from the window, he held his coffee cup in salute and grinned. Then, pointing at her car, he motioned for her to come join him on the lawn.

Nodding, Hayley signaled that she'd be out in a minute, then ran to the bathroom for a fast shower. Quickly drying her hair, she twisted it into a loose ponytail at the top of her head, then hopped into a pair of cutoff jeans and an old sweatshirt.

He was still here! She'd been positive last night, as she lay tossing and turning in bed after the embarrassing encounter on the porch, that he'd have opted to call in his chips on this birthday farce and hit the road. But, much to her mutual trepidation and relief, he was still here. Emotions warred within as she put the finishing touches on her makeup. What was she going to do with him? What was she going to do when he left? Stopping, she stared at her reflection in the mirror.

"Loosen up," she admonished, pointing her hairbrush at the woman who stared back from the pane of glass that adorned her medicine cabinet. "You're always griping about how boring your life is, yet when Mercedes gives you something exciting to do, you don't know what to make of it. Just chill out," she commanded, giving herself a fearsome scowl. That settled, she took a deep, cleansing breath and headed for the kitchen. Grabbing a cup of GT's freshly perked coffee, Hayley dashed through the house and joined him outside.

She hated herself for the giddy bubbles of joy that surged through her stomach at the sight of him, but she couldn't help herself. Like metal to a magnet, she was drawn to this mysterious man. She could only hope that once the mystery was solved and she knew him for the mortal man he really was, the attraction would end. Life was too short to spend time pining away over something she couldn't have.

Commanding herself to appear as sophisticated as she could, she moved across the porch and down the stairs over to where he stood with Old Trusty. "Hi," she called breezily, trying to mask her feelings of nervous self-consciousness about last night's kiss.

"Hi," he replied with an easy grin, setting her at ease.

Her gaze traveled from his welcoming smile over to where Old Trusty sat, idling doggedly in her driveway. "How did you get my car back to the house?" she asked curiously. "I thought he was still at the beach dead as a doornail."

"It was no problem. Just a dead battery. I found your spare set of keys under the bumper, then I jumped your car with the cab and drove your car back."

He'd done all that for her? After the monumental fool she'd made out of herself last night? Maybe all was not lost, she thought hopefully. Maybe they could salvage the friendship. She would love that. She'd never met a man quite like GT. Looking up and down the street, she searched for his bright yellow taxi, but found only the motorcycle he'd ridden yesterday parked in her side yard.

"Where's your cab?" she asked, injecting what she hoped sounded like the right touch of friendly concern.

"Still at the beach. I thought you could take me back later to pick it up."

He turned hopeful eyes on her, as though nothing was amiss. Good, she thought with relief. If fraternizing with the client was taboo, then she could understand, she thought charitably, thankful that he didn't deem it necessary to broach old rule 311 again. It didn't take a house to fall on her for her to get the point. No matter how attracted to him she might be, she would keep him at arm's length. She could do it. Her eyes strayed of their own accord to his sun-kissed chest as he stretched and yawned. She bit her bottom lip. It wouldn't be easy, but she could do it.

"That is—" he yawned again and winked at her through his sleepy eyes "—if it fits into your schedule."

"Sure, it's no trouble. I didn't have that many plans for today, anyway," she said, taking a sip of her coffee. "You know, you didn't have to do this." She smiled ruefully and nodded at the car. "But I want you to know that I sure appreciate your going above and beyond the call of duty. I'll have to tell Mercedes what a great, uh...genie you've been."

He looked at her and shrugged. "Hey, it's no big deal. I have to be here till you use your seventh wish, anyway, so I may as well make myself useful. By the way, I changed your oil and your points and plugs. Later, when I have time, I'll give it the works. When was the last time you had this thing tuned up, anyway?"

"I, uh...can't remember," she admitted sheepishly. He was still sticking with the genie charade, hmm? she wondered idly. Golly, just how much money did Mercedes pay him? Maybe she had some other people in the office chip in. Of course. That must be it. The gals in the Data Processing pool would probably all be waiting with bated breath for her to come in and tell them about her kooky weekend with her own personal genie. What a bunch of maniacs.

"You should really take better care of your car," GT admonished, pointing a thumb under her hood. "In this day and age, you need a car you can count on."

"Okay." She knew he was right. "Where did you learn to fix cars?" she asked, gesturing to Old Trusty as GT wandered over to the driver's side window, reached in and shut off the engine. "The skills it takes to do your job seem never-ending." It was true. She wouldn't be at all surprised if he volunteered to knit a garage for her that afternoon.

He shrugged easily and pushed himself away from the car door. "You could say that."

"Well, I guess this will save me from having to wish for a new car," she joked.

"True. If you take the time to do a little preventative maintenance now and then, Old Trusty here should last for quite a while."

Hayley frowned. How did he know she called her car Old Trusty? She worried her bottom lip with her teeth. Must have overheard her use her pet name. But when?

GT's voice intruded on her ruminations. "Hey, speaking of your next wish, have you given any thought to what you might want?" Absently scratching his chest, he waited expectantly for her reply.

Hayley shook her head and rolled her eyes at the white, billowy clouds that floated lazily across the blue California sky. Would he ever get tired of this game? "No," she said, and gestured toward the house. "Why don't I fix us some breakfast and we'll discuss it?" It was the least she could do for him, after he'd spent the morning fixing her car.

"Okay," he agreed, and began picking his tools up off the ground and tossing them into his toolbox. "I'll be there in a second," he called as she headed into the house. "Say, would you mind if I took a shower in your bathroom?"

"No, help yourself." Angling her head back over her shoulder, Hayley grinned. "What's wrong? Don't you have any plumbing in that bottle of yours?"

"Yes," he said, ignoring her smart-aleck remark and, planting his hands on his hips, arched a playful brow. "But it just so happens that I left it at the beach in the trunk of my cab."

It felt strange and wonderful to have a man singing in her shower, Hayley thought, listening to GT belt out his version of "A Whole New World" as she prepared breakfast for them. How corny. And yet, he had a very nice voice. No doubt when he wasn't flying planes or fixing cars or driving a cab, he juggled some kind of musical career. He certainly had the talent. And the looks.

No! She gave herself a mental kick in the seat. She had to stop thinking like that. Squelching the mental images of him drying off his fabulous body, not more than ten feet away behind her bathroom door, she fished the French toast out of the frying pan and popped it into the oven to keep it warm.

The bacon hissed and popped as she dropped it into the heated pan and pushed it around with a fork. Hopefully, GT liked a big breakfast. It was her favorite meal of the day. Making her way to the refrigerator, she pulled out a carton of eggs, and suddenly remembered that GT had told her to be thinking about what she wanted for her next wish.

That was ridiculous, she thought, clutching the eggs to her chest as she leaned against the countertop and stared off into space. He'd already done enough for her. Just getting Old Trusty in working condition again was a minor miracle in itself. Not to mention the gourmet dinner, the trip to the restaurant and the fact that he saved her from jumping out of a plane after Fred.

Maybe she should call Mercedes and tell her to let him off the hook.

"Something sure smells good," GT said, sniffing the air appreciatively as he came into the room, wearing her pink terry-cloth bathrobe and drying his hair with a hand towel. "Hope you don't mind." He slipped his thumb under the lapel of her robe.

Hayley felt her mouth go dry. *Aloof,* she cautioned her wayward libido. *Remain cool and aloof.* "Uh, sure," she squeaked, and turned quickly back to the stove, disgusted with her inability to play it cool in his presence. Good heavens, did he have to look so terrific in her pink robe? she wondered, pulling the pan off the fire and draining the grease into a bowl.

"Mmm," GT hummed into her ear as he stood over her shoulder and fished a piece of bacon out of the pan with the fork. "Perfect," he sighed. "Just the way I like it."

Taking a deep, steadying breath, Hayley smiled brightly up at him. "Great. Have a seat. Everything's ready." Okay, so she wasn't sounding exactly cool or aloof, but she wasn't sagging back against the big pink fuzzy wall of his broad chest, either. The French toast was piping hot as she removed it from the oven and set it next to the bacon.

Pulling up a stool at the island counter, Hayley perched across from GT and watched as he loaded his plate and began to eat with gusto.

"Feel free to use your fingers if you find silverware . . . inhibiting," she teased, referring to their dinner at Sultan's.

GT grinned. "That's okay. It's no fun unless you're sitting on the floor, eating Middle Eastern cuisine." Leaning on his elbows, he let his fork dangle from his fingertips as he studied her face. "So, have you given any more thought to your next wish?"

Hayley took a deep breath. "Yes."

"Great. What'll it be?"

"I think I'm going to call Mercedes and have her let you off the hook. Really. This has been a lot of fun and all, but I'm sure you have other things you could be doing, and I...uh, well, I do, too." In truth, she didn't have anything pressing to do, but he'd done enough for her. Mercedes' clever gift had been great, but enough was enough. Any more would be...embarrassing.

GT sighed, his fork clattering to his plate as he leaned back on his stool and crossed his arms over his chest. The robe drooped open, and Hayley quickly averted her eyes and pretended fascination with the syrup bottle.

"Hayley, I thought I'd made myself clear. I can't go home until you've wished all your wishes." Drawing his brows together pensively, he continued. "So, if you want to get rid of me that badly, you're just going to have to make a few wishes. Then I'll get out of your hair. But not until then," he said, his firm tone brooking no argument.

Hayley shook her head, grumpy now. He could go home if he wanted to, she thought churlishly. But no. He had to fulfill some silly contractual obligation to her friends and co-workers. It was humiliating to have him hanging around this way, when he knew damn good and well that she had a schoolgirl crush on him. He was only tolerating her because he owed Mercedes. She sighed. If he wasn't going to leave, she may as well get Mercedes' money's worth.

Wetting her bottom lip with the tip of her tongue, she pondered her options. She'd already wished for a man and that hadn't worked out. Pushing her now-cold French toast around on her plate, she glanced up at GT, who was still waiting for her to make up her mind. She wiped her mouth with her napkin and glared at him. How was she supposed to think with him staring at her that way?

Closing her eyes, she ignored him.

Maybe the reason her first wish hadn't worked—aside from the fact that GT wasn't a real genie—was because she'd wished for the wrong trait. Adventure was obviously not the kind of thing she was looking for in a long-term relationship. Hmm. Perhaps another of the four qualities she found admirable in a man would be worth exploring. After all, surely not *all* of GT's friends were as nutty as old Freddy.

Out of the three remaining qualities—self-confidence, humor and creativity—Hayley thought that self-confidence would probably be the most down-to-earth. It certainly sounded safe enough.

"Well?" GT's voice brought her eyes slowly open.

She laughed.

"What?" he asked, grinning.

"I don't know how you expect me to take you seriously when you're sitting there, uh... bursting out of my pink robe."

He frowned defensively. "I told you, my stuff's in the cab."

Giggling, Hayley shook her head. "You mean I have to drive you to the beach in that getup?"

"Just shut up and wish, will you?" he said good-naturedly.

"Okay, but I'm warning you, if this next wish is as scary as Fred Peabody was, there will be hell to pay."

GT nodded. "Message received," he said affably. "Are you going to wish for a new job this time?"

Snorting, Hayley reached for the coffeepot and refilled their cups. "No. I know you can't get me a new job. But I'm banking on the fact that you have some friends you can set me up with. Good-looking friends," she amended. "I'm still interested in finding a life partner and a father for my yet-to-be-born children," she chirped, "so, I think I'm going to go for the man again."

GT scowled. "I thought you said looks weren't important to you."

Feeling her cheeks flare, Hayley said, "They aren't. But come on, GT, surely you can do better than Fred."

"Just make your wish," he ordered, casting his eyes up then settling them on her.

"Okay." Hayley's gaze shot straight to his. "I *wish* for a nice-looking, self-confident man."

"Self-confident?" GT asked.

"And handsome," she reminded him.

"How handsome?" His eyes narrowed.

Waving an impatient hand, Hayley shook her head. "I don't know. Handsome."

Dragging a hand through his still-damp hair, he sighed. "Granted," he said somewhat irritably. What if she decided she liked this handsome guy? What if she decided to give Mr. Self-Confident Prettyboy one of those mind-blowing kisses that had kept him awake all night? He pinched the bridge of his nose between his thumb and forefinger. Then again, what the hell did he care? He was here to do a job. Rule 311, he reminded himself.

The doorbell chimed. Hayley set her coffee cup down and looked curiously at GT. "Who could that be?" she mused aloud.

"Hope you won't mind if I don't skip out and get that for you," he said sarcastically. "I'm just going to use your bathroom to slip into—" he paused dramatically, teasing her "—something a little more comfortable."

"I thought your stuff was at the beach," she called over her shoulder on her way to the door.

"It is," he called back, heading into the bathroom. "I'll just put on my jeans again for now."

Pausing at the hall mirror, Hayley looked at her reflection and pushed her hair out of her eyes. "Anything but those blasted jeans," she whispered to herself. She couldn't think straight when he wore nothing but those tight jeans.

Pasting a smile on her face, she pulled open her door, only to find a strange man on her porch studying his reflection in her doorknob.

Glancing up, he cocked an arrogant brow. "Hi, babe. You ready?" he asked, parting his perfectly formed lips and flashing her a brilliant, sparkling smile.

"Ready?" Hayley asked, staring in confusion at the muscle-bound hulk that towered in front of her. The man was positively covered with deeply tanned, bulging muscles. Even his muscles seemed to have muscles, and if Hayley didn't know better, she would swear that his earlobes were tanned and muscular. This quivering mountain of oiled, flexing flesh stood expectantly, as though waiting for her to join him for some sort of outing.

But just who was this shirtless Mr. America contender, with the obscenely tight sweatpants and a T-shirt rolled and tied around his sun-bleached, buzz-cut head? Had they met before?

"Yeah." Brushing past her into the house, he spotted the hallway mirror and began to preen in earnest. "We'd better get rollin' if I'm going to get my whole routine in. I'm workin' a split. Saturday it's arms, chest and back." He flexed his pectorals experimentally and watched them bounce with satisfaction in the mirror.

Gracious, Hayley thought, appalled and fascinated at the same time. "I'm sorry," she told him, her brow puckered in consternation, "I'm not sure I know what you're talking about."

The hulk changed his pose to best display the ripples and veins that ran across his chest and shoulders and quirked his lips haughtily. "The gym, babe," he grunted with his efforts, "the gym."

Hayley turned at the sound of GT padding down the hallway to join them.

"Hi," GT called to the strange man who stood in her foyer. "I'm GT," he said, holding his hand out in greeting, "her brother."

"Whoa, dude. I'm Ken Franklin," the muscle-bound man replied, grabbing GT's hand and pumping hard. Ken looked at Hayley. "I can see the resemblance."

GT glanced impishly over at Hayley then down at his hand. "Thanks," he said, shaking it to get the blood flowing again. "People say that about us all the time, right, sis?" He ruffled her hair affectionately.

"Oh, right." Hayley looked at GT with murder in her eyes. Was this his idea of granting her another wish? For pity's sake, she'd said handsome, not plastic. And self-confidence? Ken's picture surely rippled across a page of the dictionary under this word.

"Great." Ken looked GT up and down. "Hey, you work out, dude? If you don't, you should. You got a natural build for it. With a little fine-tuning, you could really be ripped. Like me."

GT shrugged. "I'll take that under advisement," he said, hooking his thumbs through his belt loops and winking at Hayley. "Well, anyway, you two maniacs have a good workout at the gym." He shooed them toward the door.

"Just a sec," Ken said, looking at Hayley's reflection in the mirror. "You're not going to wear that, are you, babe? Denim doesn't breathe, babe. We're gonna work up a sweat, if you know what I mean. Better grab one of those stretchy little numbers that mold to the body."

Hayley looked down at her cutoffs and sweatshirt and sighed. "Okay. I'll just get my bag and I can change at the gym." Elbowing GT rudely out of the way, she reached into her hall closet.

This was just too doggone much coincidence, she thought, rummaging around in her hall closet trying to find her seldom-used gym bag. How on earth had GT done it? And so fast? Was he using some kind of electronic communication device that allowed him to send messages to his company and instruct them regarding his needs?

Impossible. But how in blue blazes he could have managed to get Ken over to her house so quickly was beyond her. From the time she'd made her wish, to the time the doorbell rang, not more than a minute could have passed.

Could there actually be something to his outlandish story? Could he really be a genie? Were there such things? Just because she'd never met one personally, did that mean they didn't exist? After all, people had been telling the tales of wish-granting genies for literally hundreds of years. Perhaps there really was a basis for these stories.

It just went against the more practical, pragmatic side of her nature to indulge in such fantasy. But, the more she watched GT at work, the more she was beginning to believe. There certainly didn't seem to be any other explanation. As soon as she got a chance, she was going to call Mercedes and demand the truth. Until then, she thought, finally locating her dusty gym bag in the corner of her closet, she would try to get to know Ken. Perhaps get a feeling about his plans for the future. His plans for a career and family. Maybe the walking relief map that stood admiring his reflection in her foyer mirror had a deeper side. After all, she'd made a vow to stop being so picky. She should probably start with Ken. Straightening, she backed out of the dark closet and stopped. She sagged woefully as she found Ken blowing kisses at his reflection.

Eyes narrow, she glared at GT. "I'll see you later, brother dear," she hissed, sarcasm dripping from her voice.

GT smiled with wide-eyed innocence. "You kids have fun."

Aside from the fact that Ken couldn't seem to tear his eyes away from his reflection in the rearview mirror, the ride to the gym was relatively uneventful. At least, Hayley thought with relief, they'd managed to make it in one piece. However, as far as sterling conversation went, Ken was pretty much limited to himself. And his muscles. Hayley sighed.

Perhaps she should think about scratching self-confidence off the list of attributes she found attractive in a man, she mused as Ken pulled her out of his flashy sports car and into the No Fat City deli that was connected to the gym he frequented. And though masses of muscles weren't on her list, maybe she would add them, just so she could have the pleasure of scratching them off, too.

"Hope you like health food," Ken brayed over his muscular shoulder, leading her around the juice bar, past the salad bar and toward the tofu bar, where he selected a table near a mirrored wall. After they were settled across from each other in the cherry red leather booth, Ken managed to tear his loving gaze away from himself long enough to glance at Hayley. "Mind if I ask you a question?"

Finally! Hayley thought, a glimmer of hope flickering in the candle of her mind. Perhaps he'd noticed she was alive. "Shoot," she invited, smiling warmly.

"Do you think my pectorals are big enough?" He looked curiously down at his heaving bosom.

Hayley followed his eyes to his smooth-shaven chest. From there her gaze wandered to her own chest and then back over to his. "Oh, yes," she decided. "Definitely." She didn't know many women who enjoyed dating men who had better cleavage than they themselves did.

"I've been thinking," he mused thoughtfully, his eyes straying back to his reflected image as he idly flexed his biceps. "I think I need a little more definition right here." He pointed to a minuscule area between the muscle in question and his arm joint. "I bet some overhanded curls would take care of that." His eyes glazed over as he lapsed into a self-induced fitness trance.

Hayley looked blankly at his arm. If she were to hazard a guess, overhanded curls had nothing to do with his hair. Not that she was interested enough to ask. Gracious. This social moron was one of GT's friends? She was going to have to have a little talk with him about some of his buddies. Perhaps he didn't realize just how strange they really were.

"Hmm." Hayley nodded noncommittally at his muscle.

Reading her response as approval, Ken's eyes refocused and he beamed. "So, babe," he said, actually looking at her for a moment. "What are you doing clear over there?" Using one hand, he lifted the stainless-steel table by the pole and slid over to join Hayley on her side of the booth. "It was lonely over there," he said, pouting, and set the table smoothly back down before his eyes strayed back to the mirror.

"Hi. Are you two ready to order yet?" a familiar voice asked, arriving at the table. Hayley craned her neck, straining to see around the narcissistic hulk at her side, and stiffened with shock as her gaze collided with a pair of familiar fathomless black eyes.

"Whoa, babe, why didn't you tell me that your brother worked here?"

Chapter Six

GT was their waiter? Hayley stared up at him in surprise. What was *he* doing here? she wondered as he winked that infernal heart-stoppingly sexy wink of his. And when, in heaven's name, did he find time to wait tables? She glanced over at her date.

"I didn't tell you because I...uh..." she stammered, and looked suspiciously back at GT, "well, I..."

Ken seemed not to notice that she hadn't finished her explanation. "You don't want to work out on an empty stomach, babe. You should probably carbo-load before we get started," he suggested, as though she didn't have a brain of her own.

"Actually, Ken, I just had breakfast...."

He cut her off again. "Give us each a carbo pump and protein powder veggie burger, dude," Ken ordered, and turning his attention to his chest, amused himself with his dancing pecs.

"Gotcha," GT said, his eyes twinkling devilishly as he jotted their order down on his pad.

A slow burn began to spark in Hayley's midsection. Daggers of anger shot from her eyes as she squinted at GT, who in turn looked—with sudden guilty interest—at his order pad. Some genie he was turning out to be. Where did he come up with these losers? "Uh, excuse me—" Hayley tapped Ken on his granite shoulder "—I need to use the...uh..."

"Use the pot? Sure, babe." Picking Hayley up as though she were nothing but a small child, he ignored her indignant squeals of protest and lifted her over his head. His hands cradled her bottom as he placed her safely on the floor.

Landing on GT's foot, Hayley ground her heel into his toes and whispered, "I need a word with you, *brother* dear." She smiled sweetly and inclined her head with a curt nod toward the nearby rest room.

"I'll be right back with those carbo pumps," GT assured Ken, before Hayley yanked him into the bathroom. "Do you think this is such a good idea?" he asked with a curious look around, before he turned to lounge casually against the sink. "People will talk." Hooking his thumbs through his belt loops, he crossed his ankles and lifted a rakish brow.

Hayley slammed and locked the door.

"Who cares?" she cried, outraged. Spinning to face him, she battled the urge to slug him in the stomach. That would most likely wipe the cocky look off his handsome face, she thought, bunching her hands into irritated fists. "GT, where in the galloping galaxy above did you come up with that egomaniac out there? As I recall, I wished for a self-*confident* man, not a self-*centered* man!" Flipping her hair over her shoulder, she eyeballed him angrily. "You're really batting a thousand today," she ranted, pacing back and forth across the tiled floor, her eyes narrow slits of frustration.

Lifting his shoulders, GT bit back a grin. Given her present state of mind, he figured it wouldn't do to provoke her ire by making light of her complaints. He valiantly swallowed the lump of mirth that surged into his throat, and affected a sober expression.

"Maybe you should give him a chance," he suggested, encouraging her to remain open-minded. "Find out a little bit about him before you make a decision." Deep down in the recesses of his soul, he hated himself for the perverse pleasure he was taking from her reaction to Ken. Her date with old muscle-for-brains out there was failing miserably, and he couldn't have been more delighted.

Damn, man, he chided himself, realizing what he'd done. Thumping his temples with the palms of his hands, he reviewed this latest mess while Hayley stormed around the small room and vented her anger. Why couldn't he seem to give the woman what she asked for? Grimacing, he passed a hand over his jaw. If he didn't watch it, he was going to get himself suspended. It had been known to happen before. Thankfully not to him, but he was treading on thin ice here. Although, he thought—shooting a covert glance in her direction as she furiously paced a rut into the tile—for Hayley, it just might be worth it. Casting his eyes to the floor, he tried to look properly sympathetic.

"Oh, I found out everything I need to know about *him* on my way over here." Hayley waved her arms in the air. "For starters, he wants to star in, and market his own, and I'm quoting here, *Pump and Jump Body Building to Rap Music* video. Let's see, if I remember correctly, the song he wants to record goes something like this.

If you have a lump
   Or a bump in your rump
   Don't sit there like a chump
   Lookin' like a frump
Pump and Jump. Pump and Jump.''

Hayley looked with plaintive horror at GT. "And, if that doesn't work out, he says he'll settle for starring in action movies. And, this is the scariest part of all, did you know that he actually wants to be a *father* someday?" she asked incredulously.

GT worked the muscles in his jaw as he pondered her statement. The image of hammerhead Ken out there, fathering Hayley's babies, stuck in his craw. Usually he thought of the long-term ramifications of each and every wish he granted. What the hell had he been thinking this time? Obviously, when it came to Hayley Douglas, he was unable to think at all.

"I thought you said you were looking for someone who wanted to have children," GT said innocently, hoping to somehow salvage the situation. Although, he'd like nothing better than to cancel this wish and go zap Mr. Muscle out there into oblivion. The very thought of that Neanderthal sharing one of Hayley's trance-inducing kisses—let alone her children—made him want to kick down the bathroom door.

"Yes, but GT, they're not even born yet and he expects them to be perfect. No flab on his tykes. He's already designing a tiny weight set for his boys. Can you believe that? Oh, GT..." Hayley wailed and stopped pacing to gaze at him with pleading eyes. "I don't think I can finish out this wish." Tears brimmed against her lower lashes and threatened to spill down her cheeks. "He thinks my name is *Babe*, GT! I'm trying so hard to like him, but he's such a...a *boob!*"

Pushing himself away from the sink, GT moved over toward where Hayley stood by the door. "Actually," he said, biting the inside of his cheek, "he's more like...two, uh, boobs." He grinned and, bending low, peered up into her face.

Her smile was watery. "Very funny," she said, sniffing.

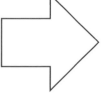

NO COST! NO OBLIGATION TO BUY!
NO PURCHASE NECESSARY!

PLAY "LUCKY 7"
AND GET FIVE FREE GIFTS!

HOW TO PLAY:

1. With a coin, carefully scratch off the silver box at the right. Then check the claim chart to see what we have for you—FREE BOOKS and a gift—ALL YOURS! ALL FREE!

2. Send back this card and you'll receive brand-new Silhouette Romance™ novels. These books have a cover price of $3.25 each, but they are yours to keep absolutely free.

3. There's no catch. You're under no obligation to buy anything. We charge nothing—ZERO—for your first shipment. And you don't have to make any minimum number of purchases—not even one!

4. The fact is thousands of readers enjoy receiving books by mail from the Silhouette Reader Service™ months before they're available in stores. They like the convenience of home delivery and they love our discount prices!

5. We hope that after receiving your free books you'll want to remain a subscriber. But the choice is yours—to continue or cancel, anytime at all! So why not take us up on our invitation, with no risk of any kind. You'll be glad you did!

This beautiful porcelain box is topped with a lovely bouquet of porcelain flowers, perfect for holding rings, pins or other precious trinkets — and is yours absolutely free when you accept our no risk offer!

PLAY "LUCKY 7"

**Just scratch off the silver box with a coin.
Then check below to see the gifts you get.**

YES! I have scratched off the silver box. Please send me all the gifts for which I qualify. I understand I am under no obligation to purchase any books, as explained on the back and on the opposite page.

215 CIS A3H9
(U-SIL-R-08/96)

NAME

ADDRESS   APT.

CITY   STATE   ZIP

 WORTH FOUR FREE BOOKS PLUS A FREE PORCELAIN TRINKET BOX

 WORTH THREE FREE BOOKS

 WORTH TWO FREE BOOKS

 WORTH ONE FREE BOOK

Offer limited to one per household and not valid to current Silhouette Romance™ subscribers. All orders subject to approval.

© 1990 HARLEQUIN ENTERPRISES LIMITED   **PRINTED IN U.S.A.**

THE SILHOUETTE READER SERVICE™: HERE'S HOW IT WORKS

Accepting free books places you under no obligation to buy anything. You may keep the books and gift and return the shipping statement marked "cancel". If you do not cancel, about a month later we'll send you 6 additional novels, and bill you just $2.67 each plus 25¢ delivery and applicable sales tax, if any.* That's the complete price—and compared to cover prices of $3.25 each–quite a bargain! You may cancel at any time, but if you choose to continue, every month we'll send you 6 more books, which you may either purchase at the discount price…or return to us and cancel your subscription.

*Terms and prices subject to change without notice. Sales tax applicable in N.Y.

If offer card is missing, write to: Silhouette Reader Service, 3010 Walden Ave., PO Box 1867, Buffalo, NY 14240-1867

BUSINESS REPLY MAIL
FIRST-CLASS MAIL   PERMIT NO. 717   BUFFALO, NY

POSTAGE WILL BE PAID BY ADDRESSEE

SILHOUETTE READER SERVICE
3010 WALDEN AVE
PO BOX 1867
BUFFALO NY 14240-9952

NO POSTAGE
NECESSARY
IF MAILED
IN THE
UNITED STATES

Suddenly, he felt like a first-class heel, sticking her with Ken this way. But, for the life of him, he couldn't figure out why he kept granting her wishes with losers. He liked Hayley. He wanted her to be happy. And, perhaps, therein lay the problem. Maybe he liked Hayley a little too much.

Reaching out, he traced the damp contours of her cheek with the pad of his thumb. Why couldn't he seem to control this growing attraction? If he didn't get a handle on it pretty soon, it could create a future problem with his career. And that would not be good. No. That's precisely why he liked his job so much. It was hassle-free.

On the other hand, what harm could there be in having a client for a friend? Surely he and Hayley could have a platonic friendship, couldn't they? He couldn't recall anything in the handbook against that.

"Oh, honey, I'm so sorry." Gathering her into his arms, he pulled her close and kissed the tip of her nose. "I know Ken seems somewhat self-absorbed. Why don't you go out there and tell him a little bit about yourself? Maybe he'll surprise you."

"True. And maybe Dolly Parton wears a training bra, but somehow, I doubt it," she grumbled and, leaning back in his embrace, lifted her eyes to him with a smile. She sighed as he cradled her head against his chest, the steady thrum of his heart soothing her frazzled nerves. It felt so wonderful standing there, with his arms wrapped around her this way. She preferred GT's strong, hard body to Ken's quivering mountain of rippling flesh any day. Interesting how, when she stood so close to GT like this, all of her little problems seemed to disappear. Even though he probably wasn't really a genie, for her there was something magic about this mysterious man.

GT's chuckle resonated comfortingly in his chest as he stroked her hair, and Hayley burrowed deeper into the circle of his arms. Backing them up against the bathroom wall, he tipped her chin with the crook of his forefinger and looked deeply into her eyes.

"Are you going to be all right out there? I could take you home if you like."

She would like. But—as much of a bore as she found Ken to be—it went against her nature to just stand him up. "I'll be fine," she said, nodding. "Thanks, though." It was so nice to know she could always count on him to get her out of a jam.

"Sure." GT was disappointed. A small part of him had hoped that she would demand he take her home immediately. He should have known that she'd be a good sport about the whole thing. That was just one of the many things he was coming to appreciate about her. She was just as beautiful on the inside as she was on the outside.

And she was beautiful.

Lucky for him old Kenny boy was too busy staring at himself to notice just how beautiful she really was.

"*Beautiful,*" he murmured, surprised to discover he'd given voice to his thoughts.

"Pardon?" Hayley strained slightly toward him to hear better.

He knew he really shouldn't stand this close to a client. "I said—" he sighed and closed his eyes, knowing he really shouldn't admit these feelings to her "—I think you're...beautiful."

"No."

The word, a light puff of air, tickled his cheek. Framing her cheeks with his hands, he brought her lips up to his. "Yes," he said before claiming her mouth for a kiss.

It wasn't just any old genie-client-type kiss, and it certainly wasn't a friendly kiss. No, this, GT was beginning to fear as his pulse roared in his ears, was more of a kiss between lovers. The stuff that in the movies sent waves crashing up on the beach and trains roaring through tunnels.

He was losing his mind, he thought, feeling suddenly high as he drank from the intoxicating wine of her kiss. He had to stop, his mind screamed frantically, for he was afraid he was becoming hopelessly dependent on her. It was almost as if she'd somehow gotten into his system, drugging him, and he had to have more or die. Pushing her more firmly against the wall, he greedily took what she offered without a single rational thought to his future. His fate.

His . . . life.

If it hadn't been for the insistent pounding on the bathroom door, GT could only speculate what might have happened to his mortality. Chest heaving, he thrust Hayley away from him and looked at her with wild eyes. "I, uh . . . have to get back to work."

"I know," she said, looking as stunned by what had just happened as he felt. "I'm sorry, about you know, rule 310."

"Eleven."

"Whatever."

The pounding outside the door became more frantic. "Hey, hurry it up in there, will ya?"

GT squeezed Hayley's arms. "Don't be sorry," he murmured, dying a little inside. "It was my fault. I'll try not to let it happen anymore." He felt winded. Weak. As though he'd just flown in from another time zone. This time, without a plane.

Her smile faded. "Sure," she said.

GT closed his eyes to the wounded look on her face. He couldn't take it. Self-preservation uppermost in his mind, he forced himself to turn Hayley around and unlock the door. Gritting his teeth, he said, "Give Ken a chance, Hayley. Maybe, if you look deep enough, you can find a few redeeming qualities." Ruefully, he supposed if one looked hard enough at anything, one could find redeeming qualities.

* * *

An hour later, Hayley was trying her level best not to gag. "Umm, Ken?"

"Hmm?" Ken was busily downing his third carbo pump.

"What exactly is in a protein powder veggie burger?" she asked around the vile-tasting lump of mush that sat heavily on her tongue. "On second thought—" she brought her napkin to her lips and forced herself to swallow "—I don't want to know."

Ken belched comfortably and glanced at the clock. "Well, my blood sugar's up. Time to get to it," he said, and pushing the heavy table easily out of the way, dragged Hayley to her feet.

She scanned the room for GT as Ken led her through the No Fat City deli and into the gym, but he seemed to have disappeared. Great, she thought morosely. Now she was left to her own devices with Ken.

Ducking into the ladies' locker room, Hayley hid as long as she could, changing into her workout togs and arranging her hair, until finally, she could put off the inevitable no longer. Closing her eyes and taking a deep breath, she pushed open the locker room door and tiptoed out into the alien world of weight lifting.

The mirrored room was virtually teaming with sweating, grunting, flexing and posing men and women of virtually every shape and size. Workout equipment clanked and squeaked as each one embarked upon their personal quest for the perfect body. Feeling incredibly intimidated, Hayley cautiously worked her way into the room and began to search for Ken.

Unfortunately she found him over at the bench press, busily slapping some poor muscle-bound soul in the face, as the man strained to lift what looked like enough iron to erect a prison.

"*Lift it, baby!*" Ken shouted, hovering over the straining man whose beet red face seemed about to explode with his effort. Adding to the redness, Ken continued his merciless beating. "Come on, you *wimp!*" he shrieked, then catching his reflection in the mirror, stopped slapping his buddy long enough to check out the progress of his own lats.

Swallowing the wave of revulsion that surged into her throat, Hayley began to back slowly toward the door. That did it. She'd officially given Ken the benefit of the doubt. She was now ready to go home and scratch self-confidence off the dwindling list of attributes that she found appealing in a man. Handsome would bite the dust, too. Dating someone who thought he was prettier than she was, she decided, was a major turnoff.

Too busy checking out his bulging physique in the mirror, Ken didn't seem to notice that Hayley had gathered her belongings and was heading out the door. But GT did.

"Hey, where do you think you're going?" GT growled teasingly from behind the front desk.

Sighing at the ceiling, Hayley didn't even bother to wonder why GT was suddenly off duty at the deli and was now apparently busy at work passing out towels to the perspiration-soaked members of the gym. She also made a valiant effort to ignore how wonderful he looked, wearing a tight black T-shirt with the sleeves rolled up over the top of his nicely shaped biceps. The white letters on the back of the shirt read Personal Trainer.

Of course, she thought, raking her hair back over her shoulder on her way past the front desk. *It made perfect sense.* When he wasn't piloting planes, driving cabs, preparing soufflés or waiting tables, he was a personal trainer. Slinging her gym bag over her shoulder, Hayley paused at the front door and tried to adjust her workout thong to better cover her bottom. No wonder she never wore these silly things, she thought, irritated, and gave up her futile attempt at modesty. She could feel GT's bold appraisal from across the lobby, and a pink heat crawled unbidden up her neck and into her cheeks.

"I'm going out to look for the greasiest, most disgusting, artery-clogging food that money can buy. Then," she declared, defiantly ignoring the looks of horror that came her way from the room full of sprout-eaters, "I'm going to *pork out!*"

That said, she turned and pushed open the glass doors that led to the parking lot . . . where it suddenly dawned on her. She'd come with Ken.

"Wait for me," GT called, vaulting easily over the front desk. Catching up to her in the parking lot, he grabbed her arm and led her over to his motorcycle. "Here," he instructed, handing her a helmet, "put this on." He took her gym bag and stowed it into a small compartment at the back of his bike. "Where to?"

Hayley grinned. "The beach?"

A gentle smile graced his mouth. "My favorite," he murmured, and helped her onto the seat behind him. "We'll stop for something sinful and decadent along the way."

"Mmm." Hayley nodded enthusiastically. "I can't wait."

Waves thundered rhythmically against the shore, creating a pleasant musical backdrop for their impromptu beach party. Since Hayley and GT had left the gym, the afternoon hours had passed in a comfortable, hazy blur and the sun was only just now beginning to dip low in the horizon. The fire that GT built inside a small ring of rocks crackled cheerily in the twilight, and the smell of wood smoke mingled pleasantly with the ocean breezes.

Absently, Hayley stared into the flames and wondered if Ken had noticed that she'd left the weight room yet. "What do you suppose Ken is doing now?" she asked GT, angling her head to better see him as he sat next to her.

"Oh, by now I'd imagine he's up to the *N*s at least."

"*N*s?" Hayley pushed her lips together thoughtfully.

"Yeah. While you were in the locker room changing, I overheard him telling some of the guys in the weight room about the alphabet workout."

"The *alphabet* workout?"

"Uh-huh. Today for example, Ken was going to work out every body part that began with the letters *L, M, N, O* and *P.* For *N,* he was going to concentrate on his nose, neck and knees." He grinned at Hayley. "I have a feeling that Ken is spelling-challenged."

Hayley rocked back and sent her laughter sailing up into the evening sky.

"Uh-oh," GT said, pointing at the marshmallow on the end of her stick as it suddenly burst into flames. "I hate when that happens." Grinning at her in the firelight, he handed her the full bag. "Here," he said lazily, "start over."

Shaking her head, Hayley pitched her stick, marshmallow and all, onto the fire, and leaned back on the blanket that GT had conveniently brought along. "Nah—" she sighed, feeling content "—I'll pass. I'm stuffed."

GT rolled onto his back next to Hayley and closed his eyes. "Me, too," he grunted.

After they'd left the gym, GT had stopped at a supermarket on their way to the beach. Racing helter-skelter down the aisles, they'd grabbed anything and everything that had appealed to them, piling it into the shopping cart like a couple of dieters on a binge. As they stood in line, Hayley had dubiously eyed their ridiculously overflowing cart. How they were ever going to get all this food into the small compartment at the back of GT's motorcycle stymied her.

"Kippered herring?" she whispered, quirking a brow in his direction. "You have some strange ideas about junk food to eat at the beach."

Shrugging, GT grinned. "It sounded interesting at the time."

"Okay. But capers? Kumquats? Matzo balls? Pickled pigs' feet, for crying out loud? Come on." She gestured to the eclectic pile of food. "And you call yourself a gourmet chef."

"Hey, there's some pâté in there somewhere. And I got us some of those marinated artichoke hearts and smoked oysters." He winked seductively as he began to pile food on the conveyer belt. "Besides," he said defensively, holding up a jar of shiitake mushrooms, "you never know. All this stuff might be wonderful roasted over an open fire."

Hayley wrinkled her nose. "You really aren't from around here, are you."

"I've been trying to tell you that."

"Well, don't worry. Somewhere in there I got us some good old-fashioned hot dogs and chips. And marshmallows."

"Well, sure." GT pretended insult. "If you want to be just like everyone else. And just how do you propose that we roast this—" he pointed to her frozen cheesecake "—over a fire?"

"Do we have to roast everything?"

"Yep." He grinned. "With the exception of this." Lightly kissing the end of her nose, he pointed to the grocery cart. "Did you get some sunscreen?"

"It's in there somewhere."

"Good. I'll put some on you later," he promised, slipping his hand under the neck of her T-shirt and rubbing her bare shoulder.

"Okay." Hayley's skin tingled beneath his touch. So this was what he meant by sinful and decadent.

Somehow, they'd made it to the beach, kippered herring and all. They spent the afternoon playing cards and dozing, telling silly jokes and just relaxing and getting better acquainted. It was an afternoon that she would spend untold hours reliving, slaving over her keyboard at Techno-labs.

Unfortunately, Hayley thought as she sat watching two small children and their dog frolicking in the surf, the better she knew GT, the better she liked him. Instead of dwindling away as she had hoped, her crush on him was growing to monster proportions. Glancing over at his handsome face as he lay snoozing at her side, she could almost believe that they were a happy, forever kind of couple. The kids and the dog were theirs, of course, she mused thoughtfully, as the barking and cavorting trio in the distance completed her happy fantasy.

"Hey," GT whispered languidly, circling her ankle with his hand, "what are you thinking such heavy thoughts about?"

"Oh…nothing really. Just wondering what a typical day in the life of a genie is like," she said, improvising.

Chuckling, GT ran his thumb back and forth across her calf. "Well," he murmured, opening one eye and lifting a brow at her, "that would depend on the client."

Hayley moved a little closer and leaned against his bent knee. "So, tell me about some of your clients," she suggested, loving the feel of his warm hand as it caressed the back of her leg.

"Hmm," he hummed thoughtfully, propping his head up with his free hand. "Well, as you know, everyone gets seven wishes. No more. No less."

"No wishing for more wishes?" Hayley's forehead wrinkled playfully.

"Right." His nod was solemn.

"So, do I know anyone you've worked with before?"

"Sure. Although, they would deny it."

"Why?" she asked sardonically as she sifted her hands through the sand.

"Because, after I grant the seventh wish, the client loses all recollection of the whole experience."

"Everything?"

"Well, it slowly fades, actually, and he or she comes to believe that it was all just a dream."

"No." Hayley looked skeptically at him. Just a dream? How could anyone ever forget a guy like GT? she wondered. She wouldn't ever forget him, she vowed. No matter what. She'd had some pretty nutty dreams before, but never, ever anything like this. "Just a dream, huh?"

"Yep. It's best for everyone involved, really."

"Always?"

GT squinted back into the past. "I can only think of one genie and his client who were an exception to the rule."

Propping her chin on his knee, she rested her arms loosely over his legs and made herself comfortable. The smoke from the fire drifted their way for a moment until the wind shifted and sent it out to sea. "Who?"

"A buddy of mine, actually. Mortimer."

Hayley rolled her eyes at the Pacific sky and giggled. "A genie named Mortimer?"

Grinning, GT tweaked her nose. "Yes."

"What made Mortimer so different?"

"That's a good question. He fell in love with a mortal woman—a client of his—and somehow he managed to get around rule 311 and come out virtually unscathed. To this day, no one can figure out how he did it."

"Maybe he just went up to the boss and resigned," Hayley suggested, moving her head to the side so that her cheek rested on his knee. "I don't see what the big mystery is."

GT's smile was indulgent. "It's not that easy. You don't just resign. In order to be a genie, you have to be chosen from a legion of very eager, very talented young men. Then you take your solemn vows. Very serious stuff."

"What kind of vows?"

"Vows to uphold the genie credo and never take advantage of the client," he said, shooting a slightly sheepish glance up at her. "To never leave the company, that kind of thing. If a genie ever does decide to break his vows, for whatever reason, and become mortal, there is hell to pay. Major retribution from on high." A slight frown marred his brow as he reached up and lightly stroked her cheek. "Except of course for Mortimer. Morty found a loophole."

"Any idea how he did it?" she murmured, nuzzling his fingertips, wondering where Mortimer and his true love were now.

"None." His hand drifted to her shoulder and then to her hand where it rested on his knee. "I only know that when he returned to his client, he was not allowed to remember her until—" GT's eyes tangled with hers "—he fell in love with her again. As a mortal."

Hayley's eyes drifted shut and she became lost in his tale. "Then he remembered?"

GT nodded. "Then he remembered."

She released her breath in a single long sigh of relief. "Thank heavens. I mean, what if he hadn't fallen in love with her again?"

Lifting his shoulders, GT gave his head a slight shake. "It's a risky deal, all right. Both of them had to be pretty sure of their love to make it work."

Hayley shuddered involuntarily. She couldn't bear the idea of GT figuring out the loophole, then coming back only to fall in love with someone else. "GT?"

"Hmm?"

Opening her eyes, she studied him. "Do you have any guesses what the loophole might have been?"

He shook his head. "No. And you know what's strange? I don't think Morty even knew." The fire cracked and popped, attracting GT's gaze. "And, personally, I think that's the way the boss wants it. He knows that there are some beauties out here in the trenches." GT angled his head back toward her, a small smile playing at his lips. "Women who would lure us away from the service. That's why all the rules. That's why the client forgets. That's why I adhere to rule 311. It's for the best. For everyone.''

"Yeah. I guess." Hayley shrugged amiably. If he wanted her to forget him when the party was over, she guessed that would have to be fine. He would never have to know that she would carry him in a little corner of her heart for the rest of her life. Leaning forward, she brushed some sand away from GT's cheek. It was more of an excuse to touch him than any real need to clean him up. "Tell me about some of the clients I'd know," she urged, changing the subject to something lighter. Something that didn't hurt her heart quite so much.

Rolling up onto his elbow, GT's brow furrowed in thought. "Hmm. Well, let's see. You've heard of Snow White and the Seven Dwarfs?"

Hayley's clear laughter rang out over the roar of the Pacific. "You expect me to believe that Snow White wished for seven dwarfs? Give me a break.''

GT captured her hand away from his cheek and laced his fingers through hers. "No." His grin was easy. "Where did you get that idea?''

She hooted. "Okay then, what?" she asked, giggling as GT used her hand to pull her across his body.

Tugging on a lock of her hair, he said, "It was their mother who wished for them. She was very short, herself." Impish dimples bracketed his mouth. "Actually, truth be told, she didn't wish for Grumpy, but I was in a bad mood that day.''

"Ah-ha." Hayley nodded sagely. "Your lousy track record precedes you. Poor Mrs. Dwarf.''

"Hey." He feigned hurt feelings. "Six out of seven ain't bad. And one of them even went on to be a doctor. What more could she want?''

"Nothing, I guess," she said, and smiled. "Okay, who else?''

"Ever hear of the Seven Brides for Seven Brothers?''

She rolled her eyes expressively. "You?"

"The story was loosely based on one of my gigs, yes."

"Yeah, yeah, yeah."

"You don't believe me?" Rolling her over, he pinned her beneath his body and tickled her ribs.

"No!" she yelled, laughing.

"Okay, okay, I can see you need to hear about somebody a little closer to home." Flinging a leg over hers, he captured her wrists in his free hand and nuzzled her neck with his nose. "Would you believe..." he whispered confidentially into her ear, his low voice sending gooseflesh sailing down her spine, "that Liz Taylor was a client of mine?"

Twisting in his embrace, she looked up into his twinkling eyes. "What did she wish for?"

GT raised a teasing brow. "Husbands."

Hayley squealed with laughter. "And I suppose you're going to claim the seven wonders of the world, as well."

"No, that one wasn't mine." Locking his arms firmly around her waist, he drew her earlobe into his mouth and nuzzled her for a moment.

This was fun, she thought. Going along with his game sure beat the heck out of fighting it every step of the way. When she made a concentrated effort to suspend her disbelief for a moment, she could actually believe he was her genie. As the old adage she loved said: "If you can't beat 'em, join 'em." Curling comfortably across his chest, she propped her arms and studied her supposed genie.

The firelight illuminated his face, flickering gold against the handsome contours. Reaching up, she traced those rugged planes with her fingertips. Over his cheekbones, across the dimples that framed his mouth, to the sudden serious expression that graced his lips.

Who was he? How old was he? Where did he come from? Those questions and more echoed in her mind. He was older and wiser by far than the late twenties he appeared to be, she mused. GT held in his mind the wisdom of the ages, and in his heart, eternal youth.

Was this what it was like to be in love? she wondered as her heart swelled with some foreign emotion beneath her breast. But didn't that take time? Years? Months? Weeks, at least? How could she be falling in love with someone she'd only just met yesterday? With a man who'd made it clear that love was not on his personal agenda? She sighed as GT tugged a strand of her hair away from her mouth and, twisting it around his finger, lightly kissed the coil.

The only thing Hayley knew for sure to be true was that she'd never, ever felt like this about anyone before. And she couldn't imagine ever feeling this intense, bittersweet yearning for anyone again.

Was he a genie? Was she under the influence of some ancient magical spell? She had to be. It was the only explanation she could think of for her accelerated feelings toward GT. For the first time, since yesterday afternoon when she'd first laid eyes on him, Hayley began to wish in earnest that this was not just some kind of birthday hoax. She began to wish, with all her heart, that this was the real thing.

GT pulled the lock of golden hair from between his lips and pushed at the corners of her mouth with his fingertips. She was looking far too solemn. What could she be thinking? Could her thoughts parallel his own? If they did, he was in trouble. Deep trouble. He was hooked on this woman, he thought, fingers of fear tying rapid knots in his gut. What was happening to him? He'd been around the block a few million times in his rather lengthy stay on this planet, but never before had he ever reacted this way to another woman.

"Hayley," he whispered. Even the sound of her name was magic to him.

"Hmm?" she asked, refocusing her eyes and coming back from her lonely, depressing ruminations.

Aside from the fact that his feelings for her were scaring the hell out of him, GT was enjoying their day together. As far as he was concerned, this day need never end. It was perfect. Relaxing. Arousing. Comfortable. Terrifying. All the things GT loved best about life.

Closing his eyes, he inhaled deeply, filling his lungs with sea air, and wished he didn't have to move. He wanted to stay on the Southern California beach, waves pounding against the surf, the sun splashing the last dying colors of the day across the endless western sky, the warm ocean breeze caressing their faces. He wanted to stay with Hayley resting on his chest, just exactly like this, forever.

"Hmm?" Hayley asked again, a faraway look in her eyes.

"We should probably leave. It's getting late."

She sighed heavily. "I know. You're right."

They both knew, it was too late.

Chapter Seven

GT's eyes widened in surprise as Hayley slogged into her kitchen the next morning. Gone was the sparkly eyed, pink-cheeked beauty he'd forced himself to stop kissing at the door last night after they'd returned from the beach. In her place stood a watery-eyed, splotchy-cheeked, mere shadow of her former self. Listlessly shuffling across the room, she dabbed her nose with a tissue and smiled wanly at GT.

"Good borning," she croaked, her voice low and scratchy. "I'b not feeling well today, so I thought we could have buffins and bilk for breakfast. Or—" she pulled open a cupboard door and pulled out a box of cereal "—I have some of these Bonster Bunchies. They're yubby."

Shaking his head, GT strode over to her and felt her forehead with the back of his hand. "You're burning up," he muttered, and grabbed the box of Monster Munchies away from her. "And you look awful, too. Go back to your room," he instructed, setting the box down and pushing her toward the door, "and I'll bring you breakfast in bed."

Hayley waved a disoriented hand. "Non... Naaah... Naaahn... *sense!*" She sneezed noisily. "Ohh." Dabbing at her eyes with the sleeve of her pink terry-cloth robe, she tipped her chin defiantly. "I'b fine," she wheezed.

That was a lie. She was far from fine. Surely her head would split wide open from the pressure that was building between her eyes. Her throat felt like raw meat loaf, and her nose was running so badly, she was beginning to think she should alert a plumber. And what was with the elephant that had taken up residence on her chest?

Leaning against the counter, she rested from the exertion it took to fish a fresh tissue out of her pocket and dab her eyes. Too bad she didn't have enough energy to pout. Darn it, anyway, she didn't want to be sick. She wanted to spend what precious little time she had left with GT looking and feeling wonderful. Building memories to sustain her through the relationship drought from which she was currently suffering. Feeling like a little kid whose ice cream had just rolled off the cone and onto the sidewalk, she looked plaintively at GT.

"I can't go back to bed," she protested weakly. "I have things to do."

"What on earth could be so important that it couldn't wait for you to get well?" GT asked, propelling her into her bedroom and folding back the covers. Then, taking her by the arms, he gently lowered her to the mattress.

"Well," she said, sinking wearily back into bed, "for starters, I was going to sing in the church choir this borning. But—" she paused, smiling at the absurd idea "—I guess that's out. Then I thought I had to bake a couple bore wishes so that you could go hobe."

Shaking his head impatiently, GT pulled her blankets up under her chin and then sat next to her on the edge of her bed. "Not at the expense of your health. Besides, a week or two won't amount to a hill of beans in the scope of a millennium." At least he hoped not. A jolt of excitement roared down his spine. She needed him. He couldn't leave. Controlling his enthusiasm, he tried to look blasé. "I'm not in that big of a hurry."

The fact of the matter was, he was thrilled to have an excuse to stay. He'd been dreading the moment when he'd have to grant her final wish and then disappear from her life. Now, with this brief reprieve, he could hang around for a while longer, and no one would think twice about his failure to meet the deadline on this job back at headquarters.

Ignoring the niggling worries he had about getting too close to the client and how it related to his immortality, GT took her limp hand in his and squeezed.

"Our main concern here is getting you well," he said magnanimously. That, and of course, a few more clandestine moments in her arms when she was feeling better. Clearing his throat, he asked, "Where do you keep your vitamins?"

"In the bathroob. Why?"

"Because I'm going to play nurse."

"Oh, sure." Hayley laughed. "On top of everything else, now you're a nurse." Unfortunately, laughing had been a mistake. After several tortured moments of a racking cough that she was sure would dislodge a lung, she was finally able to catch her breath and speak. "You don't have to stay. I don't want to give you by gerbs. Really, I'll be fine," she assured him, waving an airy hand.

"Oh, I can see that you're just ducky," he said, his voice dripping with good-natured sarcasm. "Besides, if you will recall, I've already been exposed to your germs. On several rather delightful occasions, I might add." He lifted an insolent lip and winked at her.

Hayley's feverish cheeks flamed impossibly brighter. "I'b sorry," she lamented. "I know how anxious you are to get back. But, I think you're right. I'b in no shape to

bake a wish. In fact, unless I'b feeling a lot better toborrow, I'b going to call in sick."

GT nodded in agreement. "That's probably a good idea.
In the meantime, I'll take care of everything."

"You don't have to do that. I can call by bother."

"I thought your mom was out of town."

She frowned. "Oh. Right. But only till toborrow," she
added, brightening. "You could leave then if you wanted."
Her voice trailed off and she looked expectantly at him.

"You can't get rid of me that easily," he chided. "Besides, you know I can't leave until you've wished your last
wish, so I may as well take care of some business around
here." He smoothed a tangled lock of spun gold away from
her flushed face. "Why don't you just take a little nap, and
I'll wake you up when breakfast is ready."

"Okay." Hayley sighed and closed her heavy eyes. It was
so wonderful to have a man like GT around the house. He
would take care of everything. He always did.

"What?" Hayley cried, staring at the game board that
lay across her lap. She shook her head violently. "Holed is
not a word." Adjusting her pillows to better support her
back, she shot a narrow glare across her bed to where GT
lay sprawled on his side.

"Sure it is." He rolled his eyes. "Obviously, you're not
a golfer."

"Okay, Mr. Golf Pro, use it in a sentence," she demanded.

"Okay, uh . . . 'I holed my ball for a par.'" He grinned
triumphantly.

"I *holed* my ball?" She hooted. "Get outta town."

"Look it up."

"I think I will," she said, reaching for the dictionary.

"Just remember that if you do, and I'm right, you lose
your turn. And, just in case you've forgotten, I'm kicking

your sorry butt all over the board for the fifth time this week.''

Pausing, she let her hand rest lightly on the book. He was right. It had been four days since Hayley had gotten sick, and they'd played every board game known to mortal—and not so mortal—man. So far, this had been the only game where GT remained undefeated. And, before he went back to wherever it was he came from, she would win at least one time, or die trying, she thought grumpily.

Scowling, she asked, ''How many points is that worth?''

''With the triple-word score and the double-letter score and . . . the extra points from the word that comes off the *D* . . . let's see . . .'' GT scribbled furiously on the score pad for a moment. ''Uh, looks like seventy-two points.''

''Seventy-two?'' Hayley leaned forward. ''What is the word that comes off the *D?*''

''Doink.''

''Doink?'' Flopping back on her pillow, she howled with laughter. ''I think you're a doink.''

''True.'' He buffed his nails arrogantly on his shirt. ''But you shouldn't say that if you don't mean it,'' GT said smugly.

''Oh, yeah?'' Hayley raised her eyebrows skeptically. ''What's it mean?''

GT grinned. ''It's an ancient Persian word, loosely translated, meaning exalted, excellent and highly energetic lover.''

Hayley yanked a pillow from behind her back and threw it at him. ''Oh, sure. And how are you going to prove that?'' she asked, teasing, then suddenly wished she could pull her slipper out of her mouth.

''Well, if you need proof, I'd be only too happy. . . .''

''No!'' Hayley cried, smacking his hand away from her arm. ''Trust you to suggest messing up the board when I'm this close to winning.'' She couldn't even think about his suggestion. To him, their relationship was all a game. But unfortunately, to her, it had suddenly become dead serious.

Beating his chest playfully, he said, "Hey, I'd mess up a lot more than the board if I was going to prove myself worthy of that title, little missy."

GT seemed oblivious to the battle she waged deep in her heart. Having him sit at the end of her bed for the fourth day in a row was starting to take its toll. Her eyes swept surreptitiously over his body as he lay draped at a lazy angle across her mattress, studying his tray of little wooden letters.

He wore a pair of sawed-off sweatpants and an old T-shirt filled with moth-eaten rips and tears, that allowed for tantalizing peeks of his smooth, nicely muscled, sun-kissed flesh. Even in repose, he exuded a power that made Hayley feel safe from everything but herself. She sighed.

"Okay. I'll give it to you, but no more doinks. I mean, it's bad enough that you use words that are suspect in English, let alone ancient Middle Eastern dialects."

GT grinned knowingly, and pretended to bite her foot through the covers. "You're just jealous because I got over fifty points for *fez.*"

Giggling, Hayley squirmed to get away from the ticklish sensations. "Hey!" she gasped, "Quit it!" She kicked her feet furiously back and forth, and GT, unable to resist the challenge, got up on his hands and knees and began to chase them around the end of the bed, growling all the while. "Now look what you made me do," she squealed, laughing and pointing at the mishmash of letters that lay in a pile at the edge of the game board.

"Oh, so what? There was no way in hell that you were going to beat me, anyway," he bragged, grabbing the game board and bopping her lightly on the head. He swept the letters off her comforter and into the box, then leapt to his feet.

Hayley felt suddenly lost and lonely. "Where are you going?" she asked, hoping he would be up for a game of Shutes and Ladders. They'd already played everything else in her closet, and she knew he probably wouldn't go for a round of Mystery Dream Date. Besides, it hit a little too close to home for her own comfort.

"I'm going to bring you a bowl of chicken soup, then I thought I'd go work on the car."

A marvelous feeling of domestic tranquillity washed over her. How wonderful it must be to have a husband like GT. So capable. So confident. So completely and utterly sexy. How had she ever gotten along without him up till now?

"GT, about the chicken soup..." She punched her pillow and flopped back against the headboard. "Do I have to eat it in here? I'm tired of being in bed."

GT put the game they'd been playing on the pile with the others and turned to face her. "I know, but you'll never get well if you're up running all over the place. Hayley, I know it's boring to stay put and relax, but it's good for you."

"Well, I didn't have much choice in the matter, did I? You're the bossiest nurse I've ever had." She thrust her lower lip out. "Do you suppose I could go outside and sit in the sun?" She looked beseechingly at him. "C'mon. I'm feeling a lot better."

Putting on his sternest expression, he shook a warning finger at Hayley. "Okay, little miss, but no aerobic activity, understood?"

"Yes," she called after his retreating back, giggling with exhilaration over her improving health. Hopping out of bed, she dug her bikini out of her dresser. "Besides—" she chortled, pulling her nightgown off over the top of her head "—you're the only doink in this crowd."

"You'd better watch it," he yelled menacingly from the kitchen.

* * *

He should have told her to stay in bed, GT thought grumpily. At least that way he might actually be able to concentrate on what was going on beneath the hood of her car. As opposed to, say, what was going on beneath that brightly colored bikini.

Engrossed in a fashion magazine, Hayley lay in a hammock, her eyes shielded by a pair of sunglasses, her hair twisted in a loose knot at the nape of her neck. His eyes traveled lower. Surely, if she didn't have pneumonia yet, she would soon contract it the way she was lying out here, practically naked. He thought about going inside and getting a blanket to toss over her, more for his own well-being than hers. But the sun was high in the sky, and he found himself sweating under his own cotton T-shirt. Ripping it off over his head, he used it to mop his brow, then tossed it onto the lawn in disgust, knowing it was more than just the summer sunshine that had him sweating bullets.

Every once in a while, she would look over at him and smile invitingly, and it was all he could do to keep from leaping across the yard and jumping into that swing with her.

"How's it going?" Hayley called cheerfully, sipping on the blended fruit drink he'd made for her.

Good question, he thought, shaking his hair back out of his face and stretching. Was she referring to his progress on her car, or the havoc that skimpy swimsuit she wore was wreaking on his ability to concentrate? He glanced back at Old Trusty. At this rate, he'd be here until sometime well into the next century. "Fine," he lied, smiling casually. "Almost done."

Hayley stretched contentedly in the sunshine, and GT felt his heart skip a beat. "You're wonderful," she said and smiled again.

She might not think he was so wonderful if she had any idea what was going through his mind, he mused, turning his attention back to the car. Finally, with an effort worthy of Samson, GT managed to concentrate for the several hours it took to complete his task. Old Trusty could live up to his name once again, he thought, listening to the smoothly running engine with satisfaction. Wiping his hands on a greasy towel, he glanced over at Hayley and felt something melt in the vicinity of his heart. She was asleep.

Wandering across the yard, he drew near the tree on which the hammock was tied and looked down at her. She looked so sweet, her rosy lips curved into a slack smile, her sunglasses precariously resting at the tip of her nose. What was she dreaming of? he wondered, reaching down and smoothing her soft hair away from her face. Could she be dreaming of him? He knew that she'd starred in more than one of his dreams since they'd met.

As he stood watching her sleep, his heart swelled with a curious longing that he'd never experienced before. So powerful was this emotion, that he suddenly realized he didn't know how he was going to face his future without Hayley. All of a sudden, an eternity of zinging through time and space granting wishes for people he didn't know held no meaning. No allure. No appeal.

Nah, he told himself, rubbing the tension from the back of his neck. It was just the proximity. As soon as he got away, back to his regular routine, he'd be fine. He'd forget her. She'd forget him. Laughing a silent, rueful laugh, he drew his hand away from her hair and passed it over his jaw to still the muscles that worked there. He'd never spent this much time with a client before. This must be why he was losing his perspective. It would be all right. It had to be.

He only knew that the sooner she made her wishes, the better off he'd be.

Eyes fluttering, Hayley slowly surfaced from her dreams of GT, their two kids and the dog, and looked around her bedroom. The morning sun drenched the room in light, and she could tell without looking at the clock on her nightstand that it was already late in the day. It was uncommonly silent inside the house. Her thoughts strayed to GT. Ever since she'd gotten sick, he'd taken to sleeping on her couch. He'd probably been up for hours.

Stretching, she wiggled her toes, and felt a sudden surge of energy infuse her body. Thanks to the long nap she'd taken in the hammock yesterday afternoon, she was feeling nearly as good as new. Wondering what GT had planned for the day, she hoped that now that she was on the mend, he wouldn't make her wish her last two wishes. Not just yet, anyway. She still wasn't quite ready to say goodbye.

Pushing herself up in bed, she frowned. Usually by this time of the morning, at least since she'd been sick, GT was delivering his usual breakfast in bed. Although... her lips lifted in amusement as she remembered the previous evening. More than likely he was sleeping in, thoroughly trashed after spending several wild hours chasing her hat around the Monopoly board with his boot.

He was so fun to play games with. Actually, he was so fun to do everything with. She'd taken a week of unused sick time and, since she had GT's help, hadn't bothered to call her mother. While she was confined to bed, they had watched daytime TV till they both feared they'd suffered permanent psychological damage; had eaten several batches of cookie dough before they could manage to get it into the oven; were pleased to discover that they were compatible according to several reputable fashion magazine quizzes; had made a few prank phone calls to Mercedes at the office; and had talked and gossiped and laughed like a couple of kids on spring break.

And when GT wasn't busy amusing her, he had mowed her lawn, cleaned her gutters, fixed a loose shingle, shopped for groceries, rented and returned several wonderful old movies, and given Old Trusty a new lease on life. Hayley had never felt such a perfect connection—such ecstatic harmony—with another living soul.

Throwing back the covers, she jumped out of bed and headed toward the bathroom for a quick shower. After she'd accomplished her usual morning toiletry, she stood brushing her hair and listening for sounds of GT rousing, but there were none. Strange. They hadn't played *that* late into the night. No aroma of fresh-perked java, either. Tendrils of fear began to coil around her heart. Had he left? Dropping her hairbrush into the sink, she bolted out of the bathroom in search of GT. He couldn't have gone home, could he? Not yet, she prayed, panicking, as she ran from room to room, calling his name.

She need not have worried. For there, sprawled at an incredibly awkward angle across the couch in her living room, lay a splotchy-cheeked, watery-eyed, red-nosed GT. And to Hayley, he'd never looked better.

"Hi," she breathed with relief.

"Hi," he said, his voice hoarse and low. He lifted a limp hand in greeting. Tearing several tissues from the box, he coughed a deep bone-rattling cough and stared morosely at her.

"What's wrong?" she whispered, rushing over and perching next to him on the cushion. "You caught my cold?"

He nodded.

"I'm so sorry," she murmured, feeling his forehead with her fingertips.

"Don't be," he rasped. His lips tipped up weakly at the corners of his mouth. "I've never enjoyed catching a cold quite so much."

Hayley blushed and, flustered by the suggestive look in his eyes, began to fuss over him like a mother hen. "Well, you can't stay on my couch. I won't have it."

GT closed his eyes and swallowed. "Hayley—" he sighed heavily "—I'm sorry, but I don't have anywhere else to go."

"You most certainly do," she retorted snippily, wondering why she suddenly sounded so much like her mother, Celeste. "You'll go get into my bed this instant, and I won't hear another word about it."

With a momentous effort, GT lifted his head off the sofa's armrest and grinned devilishly. "You have no idea how long I've been waiting to hear you say that," he said, and rolling off the couch, allowed Hayley to half support, half drag him to her bed.

GT was a terrible patient.

"Hayley!" he bellowed, thrashing around in her bed. "Hayley, get in here, will ya?"

Frazzled, she appeared at the doorway and arched a tired brow. "Yes?" she inquired drolly. This had better be good. He'd had her running around like a headless chicken all day long.

He stopped thrashing and looked imploringly at her. "Will you rub my feet?"

"Rub your...*feet?*" Was he kidding? When the hell did he expect her to change his sheets, make homemade ice cream for his sore throat, read the paper to him, bathe his feverish brow and fix that pot of honey-lemon tea?

"Yesss." His moan was sorrowful as he lolled his head over to one side of the bed and bestowed his best puppy-dog eyes on her. Snaking his foot out from under the covers, he waved it in her face, wiggling his toes. "Please?"

He grinned boyishly, and Hayley's heart softened. How could she refuse that face? Besides, after the way he'd taken care of her this last week, she'd be only too happy to return the favor and give him a little foot massage.

"Umm," he groaned as she took one of his feet into her lap at the end of the bed. "That feels heavenly. Harder," he instructed.

Hayley grinned and complied.

"Slower. Ohh yess," he moaned rapturously, and closed his eyes. "Higher. To the left. Lower. Ohh, ohh, perfect. Yes, sweetheart! Don't stop!" he shouted, then trying to suppress an irrepressible grin, opened one eye and watched for her reaction. "This is heavenly. Almost better than...hmm...better than..."

"A seventy-two-point doink?" Hayley asked impishly.

"Smart aleck." GT sighed. He opened his other eye and studied her. "Hayley," he said, and tiredly rubbed his eyes, "I'm really sorry, but it's going to be a while before we get back to your wishes."

"Oh?" A party of celestial carolers struck up the Hallelujah Chorus in her mind.

"Yeah." He wiggled his foot against her lap. "My powers don't work so well when I'm sick."

"Oh?" Hayley wondered what GT would think if she got up and jumped on the bed with joy. Better not. Didn't want to seem too eager.

"Uh-huh. The Edsel was invented when I was under the weather."

"I see," Hayley said, and giggled. "In that case, let's just wait until you're feeling a little better." She pressed her thumbs into the heel of his foot with renewed vigor.

"Ohh." GT wriggled his toes with ecstasy. "You're a wonderful nurse. I think I'll keep you."

Her smile faded. If only he would.

"Aim that thing over here, will ya?" GT ordered, pointing at the sudsy area on Old Trusty's hood. "Not my feet!" he yelled, exasperated, when the spray from Hayley's hose missed its mark.

She could tell by the look on his face that he knew she'd done it on purpose. Grinning, she aimed the stream of water to the area where he pointed. Even something as uninspiring as washing the car took on a whole new flavor with GT.

The hours had turned to days, which in turn had become weeks. And now two weeks after knowing GT, Hayley still had yet to make another wish. She'd fully recovered from the virus, as had GT, but even so, neither of them had brought up the topic of her next wish. After taking care of GT for a few days, Hayley had gone back to work with a smile on her lips and a song in her heart. Mercedes and the gang at the office were still playing dumb on the birthday gag with GT, but it didn't matter. They would tell her the truth in due time. And the longer she could keep him all to herself, the better she liked it.

GT's presence in her life had many pleasing side effects. Her job, she was surprised to discover, really wasn't that bad after all. Actually, it was even kind of fun, and her supervisor—recognizing the change in her attitude—had mentioned a possible promotion in the not-too-far future. Hayley had never been happier.

Together, she and GT had spent the evenings since he'd been feeling better going to the movies, picnicking on the beach, going out to dinner, and pretty much doing up the town, just like any other young courting couple in love. Except that they weren't like any other couple Hayley knew.

GT still held true to his claim that he was only here for a short while, and once she'd wished her last wish, that would be the last of him. He still maintained that he couldn't fall in love with a mortal woman, even if his physical actions screamed just the opposite. Though the physical side of their relationship had been limited to some frustrating "accidental" kisses and caresses at the end of each day, a stolen glance, a clasped hand and a squeeze of the arm, Hayley knew she meant far more to GT than he was willing to admit. Something kept him from letting himself go emotionally. Something she didn't understand. Something he couldn't tell her.

She still didn't buy his outlandish immortality story. But whatever it was that kept him at bay, it was something she knew that he had to work out for himself.

"Hayley!" GT's startled voice lassoed her back to the present. He darted out from under her misdirected spray of water and, charging around the car, headed toward her with a mischievous look in his eye.

Uh-oh. She was in trouble now. Dropping the hose, she squealed in protest and started to run. But it was too late. With the easy momentum of a seasoned superhero, GT scooped up the hose and, not missing a beat, crashed through the bushes at the side of her house, hot on her trail. Following her to the backyard, he proceeded to soak her—as she shrieked and laughed all the while—to the skin. He grabbed her around the waist and, pulling her tightly up against his body, swung her around and directed the spray of water down the front of her blouse.

"Ahh... Ahh..." she gasped, her eyes round as the frigid water cascaded down her front. *"Noo!"* she howled with laughter and, grappling against the brick wall that was his body, tried valiantly to get away from the brunt of the shower. He was much bigger and much stronger than she was, and she knew that she would have to outwit him if she wanted to get even.

"GT!" she yelled, rubbing her eye and pretending to be in pain, "GT, stop!"

"What's wrong?" he asked, concerned, and cupped her cheek with his hand.

"Nothing, you big doink!" she cried gleefully and, yanking on the waistband of his shorts, proceeded to grab his wrist and point the hose down his pants.

GT howled in mock indignation, then, ripping his wrist out of her grasp, flung the hose across the yard and wrestled her to the ground. "I'll show you who's a doink, woman," he growled as he pinned her beneath his body and stretched out on top of her.

"Oh, sure," she yelled, arching against him and trying unsuccessfully to kick him. "I can't believe you fell for the old 'I've got something in my eye' ploy. What a goober," she teased, tossing her head in an attempt to flip the heavy strands of her water-soaked hair out of her eyes.

"Unless you want me to demonstrate what a...ah, hmm...highly excellent and exalted lover I can really be, I suggest you stop that," GT groaned, his eyes straying to her T-shirt as it lay plastered across her torso.

Hayley stilled beneath the muscular frame of his arms, and her eyes shot to his. "So, I take it the hose treatment didn't cool you down?" she asked, amused.

"Hardly," he said, his tone dry.

"Me, either," she admitted.

They lay together for a suspended moment in time, eyes locked. A current of sexual tension surged between them so intense, they were powerless to fight it. They knew they were playing with a loaded gun. A mere slip of the trigger and GT would be gone. For good. Such attraction was extremely perilous, and realizing this both terrified and excited them.

"I want to kiss you," he whispered as he hovered over her, his mouth touching hers, whisper soft.

"I know," she breathed against him. "I want you, too."

He tightened his grip on her wrists. "I shouldn't. It's dangerous."

"Why?"

"Because I have so much to lose."

His voice was filled with torment. A torment that Hayley was beginning to feel herself. She closed her eyes to the pain. "I still don't understand."

Resting his forehead against hers, he nodded. "I know. And I don't know how to explain it so that you can understand." He wished that there was some way that he could take her with him. Some way that they could be together for time and eternity. But she was mortal. And there would be hell to pay if he broke his genie vow. It couldn't be done.

Sighing, GT sat up, pulling her with him. Oh, for the love of Ali Baba, what the hell had he gotten himself into, he wondered as he looked over at Hayley. She was driving him out of his camel-loving mind. Why hadn't some lucky guy latched onto this extraordinary woman and made her his wife? Were all the males on this planet a bunch of fools? Couldn't they see what he saw? It was almost as if she'd been sequestered from the rest of the world, waiting for him all her life.

He couldn't take it anymore. He had to get out of here before there was nothing left of him.

Rolling onto his side, he studied her profile. "I think it's probably time to start talking about your next wish."

"Okay," Hayley said dully, and, staring unseeing off in space, combed her fingers through the blades of grass. "When?"

Sighing, he pinched the knotted muscles at the back of his neck. They still had two wishes to go, and as far as he was concerned, the sooner they got this over with, the better. "How about now?"

"Okay," she agreed hollowly and rose to her feet. "I'll just go put on some dry clothes, all right?"

"Sure." Propping himself up on his elbow for a moment, he watched her disappear into the house, then flopped onto his back.

Suddenly and passionately, GT hated his job.

Chapter Eight

After having changed out of her wet clothes into a simple gauzy blue sundress, Hayley joined GT in the kitchen. The Saturday afternoon sun was low in the sky, causing rays of light to create dappled shadows along the walls and windows. Hayley's ceiling fan whirred gently in the background, and from where she sat at the counter, the salty smell of the ocean danced through the open Dutch door on the back of a warm sea breeze.

If it hadn't been for the fact that she had to come up with yet another wish, Hayley would have been in seventh heaven. But, as it stood now, her heart was heavy knowing that after tonight she was just one step closer to saying goodbye to GT. And that was killing her. How did one say goodbye to the love of one's life?

She guessed she could take solace from the fact that she wasn't alone. Throughout the ages, people all over the world had been saying farewell to loved ones for no apparent reason.

"Ready?" GT asked, arranging his long frame on a stool across the counter from her.

She shot him a withering look. He just couldn't wait to get out of here, could he. Well, he could just hold his damn horses. She wanted to get it right this time.

"I'm thinking," she said, trying to keep the hurt from her voice. Waving a dismissive hand, she added, "Give me a sec, will you?" She needed time to compose herself, as well as figure out what to wish for.

"Take your time."

Time. Something she was in short supply of. She took a deep breath, then let it out slowly as she thought.

The last two wishes had been complete disasters. Unless she counted the part where GT came to the rescue on both occasions. Looking back with twenty-twenty hindsight, she could almost see why her wishes had failed. Wishing for an adventurous man had been a foolhardy idea. She should have known that adventure could spell danger. And, of course, self-confidence and good looks had been rather shallow, as well. She didn't want someone who was so wrapped up in himself that he couldn't see her.

Remembering that GT would be gone soon enough, and leave behind a gaping hole in her life—as well as her heart— she knew that she still had to try to find the perfect soul mate. And if GT himself couldn't play the part, perhaps this time he could provide the person who would. Somebody with qualities that she admired. But, of these qualities, what was left?

Only a sense of humor and creativity. Hmm, she mused, creativity sounded interesting. Sensitive. Soulful. Maybe she would get lucky and end up with a poet or a songwriter.

Oh, what was the use? Hayley wondered as she floundered in an agonizing maelstrom. She glanced up at the incredibly handsome face she'd come to know and love, and her throat ached with defeat. Whoever GT fixed her up with, it wouldn't be him. She sighed tragically. He'd ruined her for anyone else. Deciding to go ahead and get it over with, she dragged her hair away from her face and smiled sadly at him.

"Ready?" he asked.

It seemed to Hayley as though his voice held a note of melancholy. Then again, it was probably just wishful thinking on her part. "Yes."

GT folded his arms across his chest. "Shoot."

"I wish for a creative man."

Exhaling noisily, he shook his head. "You're still on the man kick, huh?"

She bristled at his judgmental expression. "Yes," she intoned sarcastically. "And this time, get it right, will you?"

"Creative, huh?"

"That's what I said."

"Handsome?"

"Not if you're going to fix me up with some brain-dead bimbo, no. You can forget that. I want someone with some sensitivity. Someone who remembers his mother on Mother's Day."

"Sensitive? Hmm." GT scratched his head thoughtfully. "An unattractive, sensitive man…with a mother and a hobby." He winced. "The very thought gives me hives."

"So? You don't have to date him. I do." Hayley grinned, her mood lightening some. This could be fun, in an offbeat, consolation-prize kind of way.

"Okay," GT agreed dubiously. "Granted."

Hayley's doorbell rang, and, startled, she jumped in her seat. Would she ever get used to the way he operated? Reaching across the counter, she patted him on the arm and decided to cast off her gloomy mood and throw herself into the spirit of the occasion. "Don't get up," she sang sweetly. "I'll get it."

"Yes," he muttered as she skipped out of the room, "I'm afraid so."

Not bothering to check her reflection in the mirror this time, she yanked open her front door to find a very frail-looking older woman stooped over on her stoop. Was this some kind of joke? she wondered, glancing back into the house at GT as he ambled down the hallway to join her.

The old lady stomped her high heel savagely on the wooden floor and pursed her gooey red lips. "Hayley Douglas?" the woman roared, her bright orange beehive hairdo bobbing precariously.

Okay, she would scratch the part about frail.

"Yes..." Hayley replied tentatively, and lifted a confused eyebrow at GT. This certainly wasn't the answer to her wish.

GT shrugged noncommittally at her silent query.

"Humph." Looking Hayley up and down through the thick lenses of her trifocals, the older woman showed disapproval on her time-weathered face. *"Walter!"* she screeched, hobbling back to the edge of the porch and motioning with her bony arms to the black stretch limousine that sat parked at the curb. "Come on, Walt!" she beckoned, clutching the porch post with her free hand. "This is the right address. You can come out now." Taking several dozen tiny steps, the strange woman about-faced and peered over the edge of her spectacles at Hayley. "Are ya gonna invite me in, or do I have to stand out here all night?" she demanded, reaching over and, like a chicken at feed time, pecked Hayley in the ribs with her brightly colored nails.

"I...why...well, of course." Hayley glanced back at GT, who nodded encouragingly.

"Of course, what?" The short-tempered woman pushed her stiffly lacquered beehive back up to the top of her head, where it apparently belonged.

"Uh, well, come in, I guess." Hayley stood back and let the old woman shuffle slowly past.

"Come on, Walt!" she bellowed, pausing at the front door to wait for the mysterious Walt.

Curiously, Hayley lifted her gaze back out to the curb to discover the most amazingly skinny skeleton of a man that she had ever seen, disentangling his lanky frame from the interior of the limousine. As he loped awkwardly around the car and up her walk, Hayley could see that he sported a stringy little goatee at the tip of his pointed chin.

An artist's cap, draped at a cockeyed angle, adorned the top of his head, and his hair was slicked back into a longish ponytail. The tuxedo jacket he wore hung loosely on his sunken chest, and was far too short in the sleeve for his gangly arms. Hunching over, as if to disguise his incredible height, he stumbled up the front porch stairs in an effort to obey the tiny dictator that shouted at him from the front door.

Hayley scowled back at GT—as he stood hovering over her shoulder—and noted with irritation the look of amusement that flashed across his face. So, he thought this was funny, did he? Jabbing him roughly in the side with her elbow, she backed up to make way for her guests. Whoever they were.

Okay, she sighed resignedly to herself as she turned to smile a greeting at Walter, technically GT had listened to her request on this wish. This man was certainly not short and fat and frenetic like Fred. Nor was he incredibly built and handsome and narcissistic like Ken.

But really, she groaned inwardly and swallowed the urge to scream.

As the thin man drew near, Hayley crossed the porch and, reaching out, grasped his clammy hand and assisted him up the stairs. "I...uh...okay...there you go," she said, trying as always to be the solicitous hostess and pointing out the porch ceiling to the taller-than-average

Walt. "Watch your head." She smiled brightly to disguise her feelings of foreboding.

Pausing next to her, he brought his scraggly chin down to her ear and purred, his moist breath hot against her cheek. "I'd rather watch yours," he said with an awkward attempt at wit, and bestowed her with a flamboyant wink.

She cringed. *This* was the sensitive, creative man of her dreams? He winked with great affectation once again, and Hayley couldn't help but stare. Trying to get a good look at him without seeming impolite, she decided that it wasn't really a wink. At least not the way GT was always winking at her with those sexy, dark bedroom eyes of his. Walt seemed to have more of an uncontrollable twitch happening there. Hayley had to force herself to stop staring at his affliction.

Reaching around Hayley, GT held his hand out in his customary style. "Hi. I'm GT. Hayley's bodyguard."

Hayley twisted back to shoot him a disgusted glance. Who in their right mind would ever believe that she needed a bodyguard? It wasn't as if she even knew how to ice skate.

Walt's eyelid went through a series of energetic gymnastics before he appeared able to speak. Taking GT's hand in a limp, ineffectual grip, the tall man quirked his lips up at the corners. "Hello. I'm *Walter Tyrnan?*" He emphasized his name as though they must know him, and didn't bother explaining his line of work. "And this—" his eyelid appeared to do a back flip "—is my mother." He gestured to the orange hair at his elbow.

Walt's mother snorted. "What are we still doin' out here? Come on, Walt," she demanded, and leading with her chin, barged past Hayley, dragging her son behind her.

Hayley and GT followed the odd couple to the living room and exchanged wide-eyed looks.

"Won't you sit down?" she invited, reticent to encourage this latest version of her future soul mate and his mother to stay but not knowing what else to do with GT's little surprise.

"Umf." Mrs. Tyrnan took the recliner.

The tick in Walt's eye jumped spastically as he unfurled his body on the love seat. Patting the cushion beside him, he motioned for Hayley to join him. "Darling, the light is perfect over here. Come sit where I can really see you." His voice was husky with an undercurrent of some emotion that Hayley couldn't bring herself to analyze.

"I...uh...okay." Hayley edged over to the love seat and perched as far away from Walt as she could.

GT, in true bodyguard form, followed and—nudging her over next to Walt—squeezed in between her and the arm-rest.

"Cool it," she whispered through her teeth as he practically forced her across Walt's lap.

"Just trying to get things rolling," he murmured into her hair, then smiled innocently at her.

The difference in the two men's bodies was amazing, Hayley thought, leaning back toward the safe haven of GT's powerful form. Where Walt was a nervously twitching pile of bones—GT was rock solid, and radiating some kind of kinetic energy that flowed from his body directly into hers. GT rested a casual arm over the back of the love seat, and, unable to help herself, Hayley nestled more snugly into his side. It wasn't as if it was her fault. For as much as GT attracted her, Walt repelled her.

"I don't know, Walt," Mrs. Tyrnan said crabbily, looking Hayley over. "She's scrawny."

Hayley's mouth dropped open, nonplussed. Scrawny? Hello? Excuse me? I'm sitting right here, she thought, churlishly, appalled at the woman's rudeness.

Winking and blinking, Walt nodded and leered down at Hayley. "Yes, but she's not that thin, Mother."

Oh. Right. Hayley bristled. *So now she was fat.* She could feel GT's body shake with silent mirth, and decided that before the evening was over she was going to kill him.

Walt's eyes roamed over her bustline.

Mrs. Tyrnan retrieved a lipstick from her purse and began to apply yet another coat of fire-engine red to her lips and the surrounding area. "Well, I suppose we could work on the body some. But I don't like the way she wears her hair. I think something upswept and more fashionable is befitting to your life-style, Walt," she ordained imperially, patting the orange road construction cone at the top of her own head.

Hayley's gritted her teeth. What life-style?

"Darling, Mother wants to have a say-so in the woman I marry," Walt explained matter-of-factly. "Because we'll be living with her after we marry."

After we marry? Too stunned to reply, Hayley swallowed and looked helplessly at GT. This wish was already worse than the other two, and it hadn't even started yet. Obviously, she and GT had some kind of communication gap when it came to her wishes. Why were they in such perfect sync on every other aspect of life? Was he trying to prove something? Could it be that he was trying to show her that wishing for a man was a bad idea?

"And another thing, Walt. I don't like the way she's dressed. Surely you have a modest evening dress," Mrs. Tyrnan said, finally directing her comments to Hayley. "You can't go to Walt's opening dressed in that silly little frock you have on." She pointed to Hayley's sundress. "Go on, now. You don't want to keep Walt waiting on his big night." She sniffed.

Hayley took the opportunity to leap to her feet. "No, I wouldn't want to keep Walt waiting on his big night." Her smile was steely as she motioned for GT to come with her. "Excuse me while I go change into something more appropriate for Walt's . . . er . . . big night," she said sweetly, and nudged GT roughly to his feet. "Could I see you for a minute?" she hissed under her breath.

"I'll just go...ah...guard her," GT explained lamely and, grinning at Walt and his mother, followed Hayley's rapidly retreating form out of the room.

"Who *are* those people?" Hayley demanded irately as she yanked GT into her bedroom. Slamming the door shut, she whirled to face him. "You can't tell me that you actually expect me to go out with that oversexed telephone pole and that human fright wig he calls Mother, do you?"

GT shrugged and ambled over to her closet. Opening the door, he began sorting through her dresses. "It won't kill you to go out with him on his big night, will it?" he asked as he rummaged around. "Here," he said triumphantly, tossing a sparkly gold sequined number into her arms. "This looks like it would be appropriate for a...big night."

"She said *modest* evening dress, GT. I don't think this is exactly what she had in mind for whatever this function is tonight. And what in blue blazes is a *big* night? Should I be getting nervous here?" Why wouldn't anybody tell her what was going on? "What's so...big about it?"

GT grinned and shook his head. "Hey, I'm immortal, not omniscient."

Hayley pursed her lips in annoyance. "Do you mean to tell me that you don't know this guy? He's not another one of your friends?" She stood staring at him, arms akimbo, the sparkly gold dress dangling from her fingertips. He expected her to go out with a *complete stranger?* Strange being the operative word in this case, she thought, fuming.

GT dragged a frustrated hand across his face. "Hayley, none of them have been my friends. I told you that a long time ago."

"Okay," she snapped, brandishing the gold dress in his face impatiently, "your co-worker. Your employee. Whatever. Who is he?"

"He is—to the best of my ability—the answer to your request."

Hayley's laugh was sharp as she tossed the dress on her bed. "Oh, pulleez. *He* is the best of your ability?"

"Hey, did I force you to ask for a funny-looking creative guy? I don't think so. That was your brainy idea, as I recall. You could have asked for something simple, like a million dollars, but noo...."

"Oh, sure. Now it's my fault that...that...weirdo and his mother are sitting out there." If she hadn't been quite so enamored with GT, she might consider filing a complaint with his boss. "GT, you must know at least *one* halfway normal person that you could fix me up with. I think you're giving me these losers on purpose!" She could tell by the defensive look on his face that she was hitting a little too close to home.

GT moved directly in front of her. His stance was wide as he crossed his arms at his chest in typical Yul Brynner fashion. "Hayley, it's a little late to go changing your mind on this deal. These people are sitting in your living room, waiting for you. It's Walt's big night. What the hell do you want me to do now?"

She looked up into his dark, brooding eyes. It was all she could do not to throw herself out the window of her one-story house. But aside from the fact that she would probably only break a nail, she couldn't bail out like that. GT was right. She may not like it, but they were counting on her to be there for whatever it was Walt and his mother were so excited about tonight.

She had to go. However, she didn't have to go alone, did she? "I want you to go with me."

Tilting his head, GT planted his hands on his hips, a bemused smile gracing his mouth. "Of course. I'd planned on it, anyway. You should know that by now."

In her heart of hearts, she did. That's what she loved about him. "Okay. I guess we can let them think that I don't go anywhere without my...bodyguard. They didn't seem to think it was odd that I have one.''

Reaching out the few short inches it took to grasp her arms, GT drew her up against his heavily beating heart. "Honey, one look at you and it's obvious this delightful body needs guarding." He ran his palms up her back and buried his fingers in her hair.

Tilting her head back into the cradle of his hands, she pretended to pout. "Don't you mean my scrawny body?"

He threw back his head and let out a peal of laughter. Then, his eyes gleaming with fun, he kissed her mouth quick and hard. "Consider the source. Walt's mother isn't my idea of a beauty consultant. I mean that orange beaver dam she's got going at the top of her head is scary enough," he teased, rubbing his nose against hers. "But when you put it together with the lipstick on her teeth, she looks like something straight out of the Freddy Kreuger school of beauty."

An unwilling giggle escaped Hayley's lips.

Pulling her against his chest, he rested his chin on the top of her head and tightened his arms at her waist. "To me, you are the perfect woman," he murmured, growing suddenly very still. "And if I wasn't in jeopardy of losing my job—" he paused, and Hayley could feel him swallow at her temple "—and my...future, I'd fall madly in love with you and beg you to marry me."

"But you can't do that."

"No. I...can't...do that."

"Well, then..." her voice trailed off miserably. She was doomed to spend her life with a meatball like Fred. Or Ken. Or...Walt. "I guess I should get dressed and get out there. I don't want to keep Walt and his mother waiting."

"No," GT agreed reluctantly. "Not on his big night." He gestured to the sequined dress she had tossed on the bed. "You wouldn't happen to need some help getting into that thing, would you?'' His eyes passed swiftly over her lithe body. She'd look great in a gunnysack.

"Thanks for the offer, but I can manage."

"Well, then, I guess I'll go...guard the door."

Just let Walt try to get past him tonight, he thought with a grim set to his jaw. He gave Hayley a proprietary kiss on the forehead and squeezed her arm reassuringly. Then, before he lost his nerve and tried to persuade her not to go out with Walt, he strode out into the hall and took up his post outside her bedroom door.

Hayley pulled at the uncomfortable bodice of her strapless, gold-sequined evening gown, and wished she had just a little more room to breathe. The sequins were scratchy, and the stays dug into her sides and stomach. Feeling Walt's lecherous stare rove over her thighs, she switched her hands to her hemline and continued her impatient tugging. The interior of the limousine seemed uncomfortably crowded, and staring at the door panel by her elbow, she wondered which of the many buttons she could push to get some air.

As though sensing her need, GT reached over from where he sat across from her, next to Walt's mother, and cracked the window. Together they took in deep breaths of fresh air and smiled at each other. Hayley was so glad he was there. She didn't think she could have taken these cramped quarters with the Tyrnans if it hadn't been for him. Especially the way Walt was crowding her. Looking over at the tongue-wagging Mrs. Tyrnan, Hayley tried to fake her way back into the conversation with a smile and an enthusiastic nod.

"...René?" Walt's mother asked, pausing for a moment in her lengthy diatribe. "You've heard of him." She'd been talking nonstop since they'd left.

Of course, Walt—who was accustomed to his mother's endless droning—had a highly developed knack for tuning out and turning on. So when Walt wasn't leaning heavily against her, his bony shoulders undulating in some sort of primal mating ritual, he was murmuring sweet nothings and blowing in her ear.

"I'm sorry." Hayley leaned away from Walt toward Mother Tyrnan. "René?" She shook her head slightly. "You were saying? I'm afraid I don't..." her voice trailed off lamely.

"You don't know who *René* is?" Mrs. Tyrnan asked, scandalized. She looked disdainfully around the limo, as if suddenly discovering she was in the presence of complete idiots. Her son included. "Why," she shouted condescendingly, "he's only one of the most famous arteests of our time! And he invited Walt to hang some of his work at the gala opening of his new show tonight. Very prestigious. Only the finest local arteests were invited to participate. Why, simply everyone's heard of René!"

Hayley glanced over at GT, who looked just as befuddled as she felt. Good. She wasn't the only social illiterate in the bunch.

Thankfully, they were spared any more of the pompous Mrs. Tyrnan's stage-mother routine. The limousine began to slow as it drew near the front of the new arts building downtown. A veritable mob of people was milling under the brightly lit marquee, which throbbed with the words René and Friends. Back-to-back searchlights roamed the sky, beckoning the bourgeois to come dally for a moment. Flashbulbs popped, capturing the elite as they disembarked from their chauffeured transportation.

"Walt..." Mrs. Tyrnan reached across the seat and, spitting on her handkerchief, proceeded to swab her son's face. "Now, I don't want to see you slouching, you hear me? Walt?"

As Walt's mother filled him in on the evening's etiquette, Hayley nudged GT's calf with the toe of her pump. Grinning, he closed his legs and captured her foot. The intimate gesture sent the most wonderful sensations coursing through Hayley's stomach. She tried to ignore the feel of his trousers as they whooshed softly against her stockings.

"How come I've never heard of this René person before?" she asked, leaning forward to whisper in his ear. Come to think of it, she'd never heard of this particular art gallery before, either. Or for that matter, this prestigious gala opening.

"Must be new," he whispered. GT lifted and dropped his shoulders, then shifted toward her in his seat. "To hear them talk, you'd think he was the best thing to hit the art world since Elvis on velvet."

As he grinned, Hayley could feel his breath sweet and warm against her cheek and had to resist the impulse to nuzzle his cheek with her nose. Why was it that when Walt pulled the exact same move, she was repulsed? Could it be that Walt hadn't bothered to disguise the fact he'd eaten onions for lunch? Lots of onions. No. It was definitely more than that. There was simply no comparison. GT was her dream man, and Walt . . . was her nightmare.

Not waiting for the chauffeur to assist her to the walk, Mrs. Tyrnan pushed the back door open as soon as the car slowed enough for her to escape. Dragging her son behind her, she scrambled out into the limelight. Together, she and Walt preened and posed up a storm for the paparazzi which, Hayley noticed much to her chagrin, weren't pointing their cameras at the Tyrnans.

"They're kind of sad, aren't they?" Hayley murmured to GT, who assuming the role of bodyguard, hovered at her elbow.

Grasping her arm, GT followed the Tyrnans and led her through the throng toward the large glass entryway. "Oh, I don't know. They seem to be having a good time."

It was true. Walt's mother was most definitely in her element. Smiling and waving—and at the same time hissing under her breath for Walt to stand up straight—the woman made every attempt to get her son noticed.

The cavernous, tastefully decorated art gallery was a madhouse. It seemed that Walt's mother had been right. Everyone, who was anyone, was there. A string quartet played soft chamber music in the background, and several large fountains of champagne were strategically placed hither and yon. Waiters roamed through the crowd, offering long-stemmed glasses of the bubbly golden liquid, and buffet tables, loaded with delicacies, drew long lines.

Propelling her into the throng with a light hand at the small of her back, GT moved Hayley away from Walt and his mother. Hayley couldn't be sure if it was to let Walt have his fifteen minutes in the spotlight, or if it was because he found the Tyrnans as distasteful as she did. Regardless of his motives, she was glad to be standing away from the firing line.

Hayley was relieved she'd chosen the gold-sequined gown for this evening. For it appeared that unless one was wearing either sequins, or beads or rhinestones, one was nowhere, fashionably speaking.

GT looked fabulous in his tuxedo, although how he'd been able to pull that particular rabbit out of the hat was a mystery to her. She loved the way his satin cummerbund hugged his flat stomach as he stood with his jacket pulled back, resting his hand in his trouser pocket. Her eyes drank in the breadth of his shoulders, the narrow lines of his hips. His hair and eyes were as black as the fabric of his tux, creating the enigma that was uniquely GT. He was almost too handsome to be of this earth, she mused, watching him as much at ease in this room as he had been on his motorcycle. He was 007 in a bottle. That's what he was.

Nibbling her lower lip, she decided she'd been watching too much Bond. She dragged her eyes away from GT and scanned the room till they landed on Walt and his mother and the unfortunate crowd that happened to be standing

near. Having exhausted her surrounding audience with her
incessant boasting, Walt's mother hobbled off to hound the
press, leaving her son to face the public on his own.

"Oh, Hayley, darling, I'd like you to meet a friend of
mine," Walt called loudly over the elegantly coiffed heads
of the crowd.

Hayley's cheeks burst into flame. Unwilling to call anymore attention to herself or her relationship with the bizarre Walt Tyrnan, she rushed over to his side before he
could call her name again. Grasping her hand, Walt loped,
with GT striding closely behind, over to the photogra-
phers' area.

With a clumsy wave of a gangly arm, Walt gestured to a
series of spectacular photos, obviously taken from incredible heights. Skydivers smiled happily at the camera as they
seemed to hover, free-falling above the curved surface of
the earth. Hayley stepped toward one particular picture and
felt a curious sense of recognition. *Fred?*

"Hayley, darling," Walt's husky voice flowed down over
her head and shoulders. "I'd like you to meet Fred Peabody, a good friend of mine. He's into aerial photogra-
phy. Stunts. Free-falling..." Walt moistened his lips with
the tip of his tongue, and his eyelid began to polka. "The
way one would fall for a... lover. His pictures are so exciting. Tight... Sensuous." He was fairly drooling as he
blinked at Hayley for her reaction.

GT snorted and, raking a fist through his hair, took a
step closer to Hayley. "Somebody get a hose," he muttered.

Biting the inside of her cheek, Hayley nudged his rib with
her elbow.

"Hi, doll face!" Fred cried, peering up at her with fond
recognition. Turning, he craned his neck to get a glimpse of
Walt's face, way up among the track lighting. "Hayley and
I had a thing once," he explained to Walt. Shifting his

glance back to Hayley, he took her hand in his. "I always regretted the day we broke up."

Unable to stop himself, GT reached out and touched her arm. This possessive gesture did not escape Fred's eagle eye.

"I see you brought the cable guy along, doll face."

Walt frowned. "I thought he was your bodyguard," he said, shooting a dark glance at GT.

"Uh...he is."

Fred plastered a mushy kiss across the back of Hayley's wrist. "Good to see you again, doll face," he said before hurrying off to another quadrant of the gallery to visit with other acquaintances.

A waiter passed by with a tray of champagne, and Walt snagged another glass for himself. "Come on, darling," he said huskily, and took off across the gallery, "you have to see this. I hope you find it as titillating as I do."

GT winced. "Aww, geez. I don't *even* want to know," he growled under his breath. Sighing, he rolled his eyes in disgust as Walt, taking for granted that Hayley was behind him, galloped to the other side of the room. Offering Hayley his arm, GT lifted a glass of champagne off a passing tray for her. Walt may be an up-and-coming artist, but he had the manners of a paper clip.

He didn't blame Hayley for her irritation when it came to the men he'd granted her wishes with. If he were in her shoes, he'd be mad as hell. But the ironic thing was, this time, he'd actually tried. More than anything, he'd wanted this one to be the answer to her prayers. The man of her dreams. The guy that would sweep her off her feet and into the sunset and...out of his system. It had been important that she like this guy. Extremely important. But something had gone drastically wrong in the granting process. Something he couldn't put his finger on. Couldn't seem to control.

Oh, well, he reflected, following Hayley in that damnably tight, sparkly gold dress as she threaded her way through the crowd after Walt. At least she had one more wish left. This time, he would get it right. Or die trying. Catching up with her, he slipped his hand into hers.

Walt signaled for them to join him over at the sculpture area. "Hayley, darling, over here."

Tightening her fingers imperceptibly around GT's, she hesitated for just a moment, before bravely plunging through the sea of humanity, toward Walt's voice. *What a woman,* GT thought proudly, admiring her moxie. No wonder he was having such a tough time keeping his head around her. She was everything he could ever want in a woman, and more.

GT felt his hackles begin to rise as Walt circled Hayley's waist with his snakelike arms, and proceeded to coil around her body. "Darling," he said, pulling her over to a particularly muscular sculpture in bronze. "This is the work of my dear friend René. Notice how he's captured the human body? Molded the clay in his hands...just like a...a...*lover?* Isn't it thrilling? Exciting? Sensuous?" Walt was salivating.

"For the love of Mike," GT muttered, and stepped forward to pry Hayley out of Walt's clutches. "Sponge!" he shouted to no one in particular.

Giggling, she moved forward with GT to scrutinize the piece in question. Unable to believe their eyes, they were shocked to discover that it was neither thrilling nor sensuous. *It was Ken.* They looked at each other in wide-eyed wonder.

"Babe! It's a beauty, isn't it?" Ken's voice came from directly over her shoulder, referring to the bronze likeness of himself. Turning, his gaze caught GT. "Hey, I see you brought your brother!"

"Brother?" Walt eyed them suspiciously with the eye that wasn't jumping.

"Walt! Over here, Walt!" Mrs. Tyrnan hollered from where she stood across the room, waving her bony arm and clutching some poor soul by the collar. *"Wal-ter!"*

Honing in on his mother's voice like radar, Walt simpered, "Come, darling. Mother is calling." He proceeded to traipse toward his parent without so much as a backward glance to see if they would follow.

GT raised his eyebrows rakishly at Hayley. "Mother is calling."

"And we wouldn't want to disappoint Mother." Her answering smile was impish. "Especially considering she's probably going to be my future mother-in-law."

"Not if I have anything to say about it," GT muttered, setting out after Walt.

"Pardon?" Hayley stopped and turned back to hear better.

"Nothing."

"You know," she said, giggling, trotting along behind GT, "I can see why Walt is so skinny. We haven't stopped jogging since we got here."

"Hayley, is that you?"

From somewhere amid the throng, a familiar voice rang out. Curious, Walt, Hayley and GT all stopped and searched for the source of the sound. And there she was, waving to them from where she stood near Mrs. Tyrnan.

A slow smile split Hayley's face. *"Mercedes?"*

"I'm so glad to see you," Mercedes crowed, giving her co-worker an effusive hug. "I didn't know you were coming to the gala. Why didn't you say anything at work?"

Hayley glanced at GT. "It was a last-minute decision."

"That's super! Hey, are you here to see my Owen's work?" Mercedes' head swung from Hayley to GT. "Hi," she greeted enthusiastically. "Aren't you that exotic dancer from the birthday party?"

Hayley looked over at GT, who shrugged easily.

"If you say so," he agreed.

So, she mused, they were still going to pretend that they hadn't cooked up this little genie scheme, huh? They were going to take this little ruse to the bitter end. Perhaps, once she'd wished for her last wish, Mercedes would come clean. Until then, Hayley wasn't going to waste time worrying about it. She had bigger fish to fry. Well, taller, anyway, she decided, shooting a glance up at Walt.

Walt's eye twitched back at her. "Exotic dancer?"

"Oh, yes—" Mercedes jumped in "—and a chef!" She looked with great longing at GT.

GT began to cough, and Hayley rightly suspected that it was fake. She pounded him on the back for a moment, then announced brightly, "All better. Golly, Mercedes, I didn't know Owen was an artist."

"Oh, my, yes," Mercedes said proudly, and gestured to the wall directly behind her. "He weaves baskets under water in his spare time."

Walt looked at Owen's work through a critically twitching eye. "Hayley," he began, insinuating his body between hers and GT's. His hot onion breath assailed her nostrils. "Notice the way the reeds are twined together. Like...*lovers*. Aren't they wonderful? Thrilling. Exciting." His breathing grew harder with each word. "Sensuous."

"Fruitcake," GT muttered, pushing Walt out of the way.

"Excuse me?" Walt asked pleasantly.

"Walter," Mrs. Tyrnan said, tugging on her son's sleeve. "Stay over here by your work. Some people are going to come interview you soon, so don't wander off."

Pushing his lips into a lascivious smile, Walt peeked sidelong at Hayley and then inclined his head to an area in the corner. "Hayley, darling, what do you think of my paintings?" he asked, gesturing to a series of canvases that hung on the wall near Owen's baskets.

Following Walt's gaze with her own, Hayley gripped GT's arm for support and looked into his midnight eyes, her own wide with shock. Taking a tentative step forward, they moved slightly away from Walt and stared open-mouthed at his work. Hayley couldn't remember ever having seen so many breasts in one place. Not even in the locker room at the gym where Ken worked out. Every picture was a literal tribute to the female breast.

Bringing his lips to her ear, GT whispered, "I'm beginning to think that old Walt was weaned a little too early."

Hayley clutched his lapel and tried desperately to stifle her mirth. "Don't make me laugh."

Hands held high and tipped together into a pseudo viewing frame, Walt looked lecherously in the vicinity of Hayley's bustline. "I'd love to do you."

GT took a territorial step forward, throwing an arm across her chest as though trying to shield her from a head-on collision. "Oh, I don't know about that, Walt old boy." He shook his head vehemently. "As her bodyguard, I don't think I could allow that." Turning his back on Walt, he mumbled into Hayley's neck, "Personally, I like my women with only two breasts, preferably not anywhere on the head."

Hayley choked back a laugh.

Vying for her attention, Walt moved in to grip her hand. "I'm experimenting with a new technique, and I wondered what you think...." He led her over to the corner where a single spotlight lit one of his paintings. It looked to Hayley as if he had thrown a can of paint at the canvas, then stood back to watch what happened. "I'm working with several application styles. Using the nude body as a tool." He winked frantically, then loosened his collar. "I strip down to the au naturel, and then..."

"Walter! Get over here."

Walt's head snapped guiltily around. "I'll be right back," he assured them before leaping away to find his mother.

Finally, Hayley was able to release the painful belly laugh that she'd been holding at bay. For several minutes, she and GT leaned against each other roaring with laughter and gasping for air, tears streaming down their cheeks.

"Can you believe that guy?" GT asked, mopping his face with his handkerchief.

Hayley shook her head, struggling to bring her glee under control. "Where on earth did you get him?" She whapped him on the arm.

"Earth?" he asked, looking drolly at her. "What makes you think he's from this planet?"

"That does it," she sniffed, wiping her cheeks with the back of her hand. "I'm scratching creativity off my list." She trained her liquid gaze on the black sea of GT's eyes. "And I don't mean to be rude, but I'm calling it a night."

Throwing his hands up in futility, GT buttoned his jacket and nodded. "I'll go with you."

Chapter Nine

Less than an hour later, the rhythmic clip-clop of the horse's hooves lulled Hayley into a sublime sense of well-being as she snuggled against GT. Letting her head fall back, she watched the quiet beachside park roll by from her seat in the old-fashioned carriage. Lush greenery, black now beneath the moonlight, reached out to the slowly moving vehicle, shielding it from the rest of the world. Stars twinkled high overhead with the promise of endless time and space and . . . forever.

Squeaking wooden wheels and pleasantly jangling horse rigging were the only sounds in this private oasis, aside from the steady strike of horseshoes to pavement. Lifting her face to the twinkling infinity that loomed overhead, Hayley wished that they could go on this way forever. Having GT by her side for the last few weeks had been the happiest time in her life, and knowing that it was coming to an end filled her with a bittersweet poignancy.

For who, she wondered sadly, lay ahead in the yawning chasm of her bleak future? Certainly not Walt. Or Ken. Or Fred.

And, unfortunately, not GT.

She closed her eyes as a sensation of despair swept over her and pondered her solitary option. Having one wish left was no consolation. Just look where wishes had gotten her so far. A line from a children's nursery rhyme chanted in a singsong in her mind. *If wishes were horses, beggars would ride.*

Sighing, her eyes strayed over toward GT's face and soaked up his beautiful profile while she still could. As far as genies went, he may not be much in the wish-granting category, but in every other way, he was her dream come true.

Except for the fact that he was leaving.

"I'm sorry," GT murmured to her through the darkness.

"For what?" she whispered, not moving, afraid that if she did, the spell would be broken.

Sighing heavily, he skimmed his palms along her bare shoulder and down her arm, where he laced his fingers with hers. "For the Three Stooges you've had to deal with since I came into your life."

"Four, if I count you," she teased, and shivered as he growled in her ear. "But—" her sigh echoed his own "—don't be sorry. I've learned a lot about what's important to me in a relationship."

"And what's that?" His low voice sent gooseflesh skittering down her arms.

"I think that the number one key to success is keeping your sense of humor."

GT chuckled softly. "I'd have to agree with that." He untied his bow tie and, slipping it from around his neck, handed it to her. "I'm so glad you've been able to keep yours." Forcing a deep breath impatiently from his lungs, he shook his head and began to unfasten his collar studs. "I don't know what's gotten into me. I've never had this much trouble giving a client what she wants."

"Maybe I'm just not asking for the right thing?"

"No. It's not that."

Hayley could tell he was brooding about this problem, even in the semidarkness. "GT, it doesn't matter. Really. I've had a great time."

"Me, too," he said lightly, before changing to a more serious tone. "You know you have one more wish."

Hayley flopped against him and buried her face into his chest. "Oh, please," she mumbled, "couldn't we just skip it? Haven't I been through enough?"

Tilting her chin up, he looked down into her eyes, and Hayley thought she could see her own torment reflected there. "I wish we could." He brushed a lock of her hair away from her cheek and back behind her ear. "But, you know what they say...."

"What?"

His lips lifted, a sad facsimile of a smile. "The seventh time is the charm."

"Is that what they say?" she asked dispiritedly. Her eyes strayed to an ornate street lamp as the carriage passed it by, then focused back on him. "I don't think I have the strength."

"You have to, honey. For me." Softly stroking her hair, he nudged her head to rest against his shoulder. "I can't go home if you don't."

So what? she wanted to shout. *Would that be so terrible?* But she remained stoically silent. What good would it do to nag him? He'd made his position perfectly clear from the beginning. Rule 311. There was no room in his future for her. The passing landscape grew blurry with her unshed tears.

As if he could read her mind, he kissed the top of her head and gave her a gentle squeeze. "You know I would stay if I could."

"You would?" Trying to keep the note of anguish from her voice, she smiled. She had her pride.

He seemed disturbed, and the small lines between his brow became more distinct. "In a heartbeat." Agitated, he passed a hand over his face. "But if I did, there would be trouble. Remember? We talked about that on the beach."

"What kind of trouble, exactly?" she asked, and turning, trained her gaze up at him. It couldn't be all that bad, could it?

"Galaxies would collide, planets would spin off their axes, natural and unnatural disasters." The set of his jaw was grim. "We're talking major retribution here. It's happened before—throughout the ages—with horrific results, and it's not something I want to mess with." He shook his head in frustration. "The boss does not take kindly to defection." GT's dark gaze locked with hers. "And I made a vow."

"Oh." Of course. The vow. To his boss. The soft fabric of his dinner jacket absorbed the lone tear that managed to escape past her lashes as she leaned against his shoulder.

"So, as you can see, the very least of my problems would be my own imminent death."

"Mmm." She nodded, casting her bleary eyes to the dappled gray that drew their carriage. "But, GT, nobody lives forever."

"Where I come from, they do."

"Oh." What a clever out. There was no argument for that one. How could she compete with immortality?

"No one has been able to figure out how Morty fell in love with a mortal and got away without any trouble," he mused with a shrug. "Unless you count the fact that when the time comes, he has to die." He tugged at his collar in an effort to ease the tension.

"Well, at least Mortimer has a whole lifetime together with the woman he loves." Why was she even bothering? He'd already made up his mind. He was leaving. "GT?"

"Hmm?"

"It's just that," she forged blindly ahead, "I can't envision my future without you in it."

He didn't echo her sentiment in so many words, but if, as the old adage went, actions spoke louder than words, the crushing kiss he suddenly gave her was fairly shouting it from the rooftops. His mouth moved roughly over hers, telling her of his frustration. His need. His desire. His . . . love?

Only the gentle motion of the carriage indicated that— for now, anyway—the earth was still in its proper orbit.

GT's head, however, was spinning out of control. Pulling her across his lap, he kissed her with a passion that was almost frantic in its intensity. His hands dived into her hair, and he captured her mouth beneath his, tasting her the way a man on death row would taste his last meal. He had to remember the exquisite feel of her kiss, for he had an eternity to get through without it. He knew he was crossing a line forbidden to him, but he didn't care. Suddenly, nothing else mattered. Suddenly, his considerable powers were rendered powerless, by one curvy, earthbound blonde.

Her breathing, as ragged as his own, fueled the insatiable desire that was growing like a monster in his gut. Fingers greedily explored the curve of a lip, the hollow of a cheek, the feather softness of a fringe of lashes. Over her jawline, along her silky shoulders, and around her slender waist. His hands stilled. How could he let her go? he wondered, losing his sanity as his mouth frantically plundered hers. Facing the certain void she would leave in his heart would be hell, and he knew it.

Now it was all beginning to make sense. He hadn't been able to grant her wishes for her heart's desire, because . . . she was *his* heart's desire. Fred, Ken, Walt, they were all just roadblocks he'd thrown up to keep her coming back to him. How could he give her to another man, when she was the other half of his being?

No! An angry voice shouted in his head. He had to stop now, while he still could.

Gasping, he tore his mouth from hers and thrust her at arm's length to the other side of the carriage, where he sat staring wildly at her.

"GT?"

He needed some time to think. To breathe. And he couldn't do that with Hayley looking up at him as if he was the Grinch that stole Christmas. "No." He shook his head to clear it. "I . . . can't."

"What?"

Unable to explain, he decided not to wade into that water. "You have to make your next wish." If she didn't, he was a goner.

"When?" She blinked, trying to resurface from the tidal wave that had just spit her coughing and dizzy up onto the beach.

"Tomorrow."

Tomorrow? Couldn't he see what he was putting her through, expecting her to believe this outrageous story about his immortality? But was it really so ridiculous? After every miracle he'd managed to pull off for her, there had to be some grain of truth to his story.

She only wished she could understand.

Unfortunately, she was afraid that that was one wish that even GT couldn't grant.

Squaring her shoulders, Hayley turned her eyes to his enigmatic gaze. "Okay. I'll make my last wish tomorrow."

Hayley pushed her T-bone steak back to the other side of her plate with her fork, then rearranged her asparagus into a neat pile. After carefully buttering her homemade roll, she set it on her plate and sighed. Try as she might, she just couldn't seem to choke down any of the special dinner that GT had labored over all afternoon. She knew he was only trying to help, to do something by way of a nice goodbye, but it seemed her heart had lodged permanently in her throat, making the act of swallowing impossible.

Every once in a while, he would shoot a furtive glance over at her plate and frown, as if insulted by the fact that she'd barely touched her meal. Of course, this only served to make her feel worse than she already did. And she felt just about as awful as it was possible to feel without a trip to the hospital. Unfortunately, she didn't think there was much the cardiac unit could do for her shattered heart, or she would have called 911 by now.

Covertly watching him with her peripheral vision, she noticed somewhat churlishly that there didn't seem to be anything wrong with his appetite.

Seated across from her at the kitchen's island counter, he dug into his meal as if it were his last. And, she guessed in some ways, it was. With her, anyway. She wondered absently who his next lucky client would be. Would she fall head-over-tennis-shoes in love with him, the way she had? A wave of nausea surged into her throat at the thought. She could feel him staring at her openly now and, smiling brightly at her plate to avoid a lecture, proceeded to cut her meat into hundreds of tiny pieces.

She'd spent the day alternately cursing the fact that she'd blurted her feelings out to him the night before in the carriage, and being hopeful that he would break down and return these feelings. Announce that he'd changed his mind. Decided to stay.

"Would you like a straw?" GT asked dryly.

Hayley looked up at him. "For what?"

"Your steak. You've cut it into so many pieces you could drink it."

She smiled limply. "I'm sorry."

"It's okay." Pushing himself away from the counter, he hopped to his feet. "How about a cup of coffee? I had them grind a special blend at the coffee shop this morning."

Her word came out as a heavy sigh. "Ho-kay." He'd been more solicitous than ever before all day long. Breakfast in bed, gourmet dinner, mowing the lawn, treating her like some sort of fragile Dresden doll. Unfortunately, the only thing he couldn't do was return her love.

As GT lined the coffeemaker with a fresh filter and measured the grounds, Hayley fished the piece of parchment that had come with the bottle she'd found on the beach out of her pocket. Nudging her untouched plate of food out of the way, she smoothed the wrinkled paper out on the counter and studied it.

Sure enough, there was only one little seven left in the ring of sevens that had surrounded the one big seven. Lightly, she ran her fingertips over the surface of the faded paper, searching for signs that someone had erased any of the numbers. But, finding no roughness where there had once been a circle of numerals, she pursed her lips in agitation. It was as if they had vanished into thin air.

She glanced up at GT as he strode to the sink and filled the coffeepot with water, then back down at the parchment. How did he do it? Then again, how did he do anything? Nibbling the inside of her cheek, she wondered if maybe she should just give up and believe his cockamamy story about being a magic genie. It would certainly explain everything she had no explanation for. It would also make accepting his desertion a little easier.

The aromatic scent of freshly perking coffee filled the room as GT wandered back to the counter and leaned lazily toward her from the opposite side. She wished he didn't look so wonderful, sprawled out that way, his chin propped on the palms of his hands, his biceps bulging beneath the sleeves of his T-shirt. Tiny smile lines congregated at the corners of his eyes, and the dimples that bracketed his lips deepened slightly as he lifted his onyx eyes to hers.

"What are you looking at so intently?"

She held up the paper. "I was just wondering if you knew what this big seven is for?"

Lifting it from between her thumb and forefinger, he leaned over onto one elbow and cradled his cheek with a hand. A slight frown marred his brow as he studied the markings. "Hmm—" his shoulders rose and fell lightly "—I don't really know. No one ever bothered to explain it to me, and I never asked."

"Well," Hayley said logically, "it must be there for a reason." Reaching over, she tugged at his wrist, bringing the parchment down where she could see it. The tiny hairs at the back of his forearms were soft, and the corded muscles beneath those were smooth. She'd even miss his blasted arms, she reflected morosely.

"Probably just part of the design," he said, seeming to decide that that was as good an answer as any.

"Mmm. Probably," she mused, feeling doubtful. "Do you have any idea what these other little symbols are? They look like stars and moons to me." She pointed to the crinkled edge of the paper.

"Uh-huh." GT nodded. "Those are the planets and galaxies I told you about."

"Come again?"

"You know, the ones that would spin off their axes and collide? And these symbols over here represent the natural and unnatural disasters that would occur if I didn't show up at the boss's palace by midnight, after I've granted your last wish."

Stiffening involuntarily at the mention of her last wish, she said, "Oh. Midnight, huh?" She wished she could think up a million other questions. Endless questions that would keep him there...and her heart in one piece.

"Yep. The stroke of midnight, and not a second later." Tossing the paper down by her hand, he pushed himself away from the counter and took two mugs out of the cabinet. He poured them each a cup of coffee, then sat back down on the stool across from where she sat still staring at the paper. "I hate to inconvenience you this way, but part of the deal is that the client has to put this paper—" he pointed at the parchment "—back into the bottle, then take the bottle back to the place where he or she found it no later than midnight after the final wish. So—" he lifted his mug to his lips and blew on the steamy, dark liquid "—you're going to have to go back to the beach, to the same spot you found the bottle, and throw it back into the ocean by midnight tonight."

"And if I don't?" she asked flippantly.

"The whole collision-disaster thing rolls into motion."

His expression grew ominous now, and Hayley wriggled uncomfortably in her seat. "Oh?"

"Yes. Hayley, I'm as serious as an avalanche about this. You have to swear to me that you will do this." At her look of hesitation, he repeated himself vehemently. "Swear!"

Jumping, her eyes flew to his. "I swear."

He exhaled mightily, somewhat relieved. "Good girl."

She had been unable to control the tears that had been stinging the backs of her eyes all evening, and now the dam finally broke and the flood began in earnest. She felt like a fool. First, she'd blurted out that she couldn't live without him, and now...she plucked a napkin out of the dispenser and dabbed her eyes. Now she was crying. What an idiot. Tossing the sopping napkin down on her plate, she reached for a dish towel and buried her face.

"Oh, honey." GT set his mug down and, leaping off his seat, came around the island to sweep her into his arms. Prying her face away from the towel, he kissed her damp cheeks, her suddenly pink nose, her tear-spiked lashes.

"I'm going to miss you so much," he murmured, his voice low in her ear.

He murmured soothingly for a while, words meant to comfort, but words that instead had the opposite effect. Covering her face with tiny, soft butterfly-wing kisses, he sought and found her mouth. They stood clinging to each other, kissing... and whispering... and wishing.

It was their last kiss, and they both knew it. And the feverish intensity that was building between them tore them apart, as much as it brought them together.

He clutched her with a desperation that mirrored her own, and his eyes were desolate. "If I could figure out a way to stay with you, and love you, without breaking my vows, I would do it in a heartbeat. I would give anything," he said, his voice husky with emotion, "including my life—to be with you forever. But, honey, dammit, I made a vow." He tipped her chin with a finger. "And I don't break my word. Ever." The words were agonized, filled with torment.

Resting his forehead against hers, he did internal battle with his own private demons.

"I know," she murmured, attempting to blink her tears away. Just this once, Hayley wished he was a little bit less a man of honor. However, as much as it pained her, she was forced to admire his commitment to his vows. It made her feel that if she had ever been lucky enough to marry him, he would take his vows to her very seriously. It only made her love him all the more, if possible.

He pulled her head to his chest and rested his cheek at the top of her head. "You can't be late."

"I know."

She could feel his whiskers rasp against her hair as he glanced up at the clock. "Midnight is only four hours away."

I wish for the clock to stop, she thought frantically, but knew that would do no good. "Yes," she nodded, feeling like Cinderella, knowing that at midnight she would lose her Prince Charming and turn back into the Technolabs scullery maid. "You don't have to worry. You can count on me."

His smile was lackluster. "I know I can," he said, rubbing her back, easing some of the tension from the knots he found there.

"I'm ready," she whispered finally, somewhat calmer now. The less she dragged this heinous process out, the better.

His hands stilled. "To wish?"

"Yes."

"Okay." He didn't speak for a long moment, and Hayley wondered what was going through his mind. "Shoot," he finally breathed.

Hayley had spent most of this miserable day thinking about this blasted wish. She finally decided that if there was one thing she felt confident about, it was the fact that GT wouldn't grant her another stooge. As he'd said before, the seventh time is the charm. And if he was leaving her all alone in the world in just four short hours, she wanted someone by her side as she suffered. Someone who possessed the last quality she found attractive in a man.

Extracting herself from his embrace, she stood apart from him and bravely said, "I wish for a man with a sense of humor." Because Hayley knew that if ever she needed a good laugh, it was now.

GT's eyes grew black as a raven's wing. Ever so slowly, he folded his arms across his broad chest, and after what seemed like an eternity to Hayley, nodded. "Granted," he said, and looked at her with such incredible longing it took her breath away.

The doorbell rang, and this time, Hayley didn't start. Instead, she took a deep, fortifying breath, and looked askance at GT.

"Go ahead," he urged, and winked at her with one, last heart-stoppingly sexy wink.

Frantically, she tried to memorize every detail of him as he stood there in the middle of her kitchen, the last rays of twilight streaming through the window, backlighting his powerful build. He looked truly ethereal, leveling his gaze at her beneath his dark brows.

She wondered if what he said was true, about her not remembering. Would she forget all about him, after her last wish, as he predicted? No, she vowed to herself. Somewhere, deep in her mind, the image of GT as he was now, smiling tenderly at her, burned into her memory, and she would carry it with her forever, come what may.

Turning woodenly with one last sorrow-filled look in his direction, she moved as if in a dream to the door. Checking her reflection, she was startled to discover that she still looked like a human being. Not, thankfully, the walking zombie that had suddenly possessed her body. The doorknob was cool in her hand as she twisted it to discover the latest answer to her wish.

"Hiya, sweet cheeks," Howdy Doody's evil twin thundered from just beyond her stoop. The red-faced, wiryhaired man reached for her hand and buzzed her with a palm buzzer. "Gotcha!" he cried gleefully. "Milton Grueber. At your nervous," he chortled, enjoying his idiotic pun.

Hayley spun around to give GT a piece of her mind, but he wasn't standing behind her in his typical gloating fashion. "Uh," she stammered, yanking her hand out of Bozo's viselike grip, "hang...uh, hang on a sec...will you?"

"Don't keep me waiting, sweet cheeks. We've got people to see. Places to go. Things to do." His voice followed her retreating form as she disappeared into the house.

Barreling down the hallway, she flew into the kitchen, but a quick glance around told her that he'd left the room. *GT?*

Her pulse began to roar in her ears. "GT?" she whispered, dying a little inside.

Spinning on her heel, her voice rose shrilly as she dashed through the house, searching for him. *"GT!"* After a futile search of the premises, she ran back to the kitchen as the realization finally began to sink in.

GT was gone.

Chapter Ten

Hayley pressed the button that illuminated the face of her wristwatch—not that it was necessary beneath the bright white glow of the full moon—and checked the time. There were only fifteen minutes left until midnight. Trudging barefoot through the sand, she clutched her purse and GT's barnacle-covered bottle to her chest as she made her way back to the spot where she'd first dug up the relic.

Farther up the beach, near an outcropping of rock, she could hear raucous laughter coming from a group of teenagers who were indulging in carefree horseplay around a small camp fire. Their youthful shouts were muffled by the roar of the mighty Pacific, as it ebbed and flowed.

A wide swath of light angled back across the water toward the horizon to meet the moon, and Hayley wished it were the highway to forever. For she would happily embark upon it, if it would lead her to GT. It was warm and still out here tonight, without so much as a whisper of wind. A perfect night for lovers, she thought with a catch in her throat.

Arriving at the spot where she'd found the bottle, she crossed her legs at the ankles and sank to the ground. She reached into the pocket of her white cotton summer dress and drew out a tissue and the piece of parchment that GT had told her needed to go back into the bottle.

After dabbing away the tears that had swelled into her eyes, she checked her watch again. Only thirteen minutes. Hayley took a calming breath and, smoothing the parchment over her skirt-covered knee, peered at it through the moonlight. Amazingly enough, just like all the others, the last little seven had disappeared.

"Thanks for nothing," she breathed raggedly, feeling impossibly small and bereft next to the endless expanse of the ocean. Moving the bottle into her lap, she wondered where GT was now.

"You know," she murmured, resting her chin on the ornate stopper that wobbled loosely in the neck of the bottle, "I'm really mad at you." She nodded as she imagined GT's surprised response echoing in her mind.

You are?

"Yes. I don't think it was fair of you to stick me with old Milton Grueber on our last evening together." She sniffed, wondering if she'd finally gone around the bend. Glancing over her shoulder, she looked for the men in white coats, but saw only the group of teens as they roughhoused, and was comforted somewhat by their rowdy laughter. It was the one normal thing in her world at the moment.

Sorry.

"You should be. He was everything his name implied," she continued, hoping that talking to GT this way would somehow be therapeutic. "First of all, when I couldn't find you, I went back out to the front porch, thinking you'd be there, laughing at me as usual. But you were gone." *Taking my heart with you,* she thought, but didn't say aloud. "My only consolation was that Milton had disappeared, too."

Hayley could almost fancy that she heard a chuckle rumble above the steady sigh of the sea.

She smoothed some errant strands of her hair back to the clip that held it in place. "I'm glad you can see the humor in this. However, it will be a while before I am able to laugh, I'm sure," she said, looking ruefully down at her soiled dress.

"It was such a relief to find him gone." She held the bottle out and regarded it with a beleaguered expression. "At least I had that much to be thankful for. But after I'd closed and locked the front door, I saw something move in the living room. At first I thought it was you and I was so happy, until—"

Milton?

"You guessed it. He was turning all the pictures on my wall upside down. This, of course, after he'd already run through the house short-sheeting my bed and plastic wrapping my toilet seat." She gave the bottle a scolding snap with her thumb and forefinger. "If you hadn't left on your own accord tonight, I'd have been only too happy to throw you out of the house for that one."

That wasn't really true, but it sounded dramatic, and right now, she felt very dramatic. "You'll never believe what I went through with that man tonight."

Tell me.

Amazing how it felt as though he were sitting there next to her. "Well, he had every kind of obnoxious gag in the book. He started out by inviting me to sit down next to him on the couch. Little did I know he'd planted a whoopee cushion." Leaning back, she rolled her eyes at the star-filled sky. "I hate those stupid things," she moaned plaintively.

"Then, when my face finally cooled from a four-alarm fire to a three-, he had me screaming over a pile of plastic vomit he'd tossed into the middle of the floor."

You fell for that?

"It looked *real*, GT," she cried, then feeling suddenly foolish, glanced over at the teen beach party. Thankfully, they were paying her no mind. "After that, I know I should have thrown him out, but I was so shell-shocked at finding you gone, I let him drag me to a fancy pie shop where he proceeded to humiliate me in front of the patronage by flicking the meringue from his pie at the ceiling with his spoon."

Like a cymbal clash at the end of a rim shot, a giant wave hit a boulder on the surf and sent the sea spray flying high into the night.

"They will never be able to clean that mess up," she groaned. "I'm just surprised that they didn't toss us out on our ears." Scrunching her eyes closed against the memories, she rocked forward and shook her head. "Especially the way Milton yelled across the room at some young waitress, 'Hey, aren't you the woman who had my love child?' I think the poor girl wished the floor would open up and swallow her whole." Hayley shook her head at the memory. "I wished it would swallow Milton, but unfortunately, I was fresh out of wishes.

"I kept looking around for you, hoping you'd show up and rescue me, the way you always do...." Hayley swiped at the annoying trickle of tears that slid down her cheeks. Her head was beginning to ache. "Oh, GT. Couldn't you have left me with a man who had a normal sense of humor?"

Listening, she strained to hear the echo of his voice in the roar of the tide, but all was silent except for the breakers as they steadily pounded the shore. Sighing reflectively, she continued, "I would have been happy with any of those people, if only they'd been less...flamboyant."

She blew her nose and glanced at her watch. *Five minutes.* Her stomach clenched, and she bit back a sob that surged into her throat. "I would just love," she murmured down to the bottle, "to find a simple guy who could laugh at himself and at the same time make me laugh. Someone who has a lust for life, but who wouldn't recklessly risk his life. Someone who was self-confident enough to handle any situation, but not arrogant about it. Someone who had the creativity to make life interesting . . ."

Her head dropped back against her shoulders as she stared out at the expansive void of the solar system. The infinite void that matched the hole in her heart.

"Someone," she whispered, her voice leaden with pain and yearning, "like . . . you."

Stretching her knees out in front of her, she bunched her skirt into a wad, buried her face in its soft folds, and wondered if she'd ever be able to stop crying. The ocean would surely overflow with her anguished tears.

"You know—" her lips moved against the fabric "—I'm really mad at you. I don't feel like you granted any of my wishes at all. In fact, I feel lonelier now than before I met you."

A slight wind picked up, skiffing off the cool surface of the sea, caressing her, teasing the stray tendrils at the side of her head. She lifted her face to it, holding her breath.

It was true. Before she'd met GT, she'd never fully understood how vacant her life really was. She knew that her job was unfulfilling, and her social life somewhat lackluster. But until she'd fallen in love, she'd had no idea how breathtakingly brilliant just living could be.

And, for that, she would be eternally grateful to him.

Checking her watch again, she could see that there were only two minutes left until destiny took its course. Two minutes to tell GT just how much he'd done for her. Two minutes to tell him about a lifetime's worth of love she would carry with her because of him. Two minutes simply wasn't enough time, she thought, feeling the panic begin to clutch at her weary heart.

She set the bottle down into the sand and lifted the small piece of parchment off her lap. Tenderly, she ran her fingers over the worn and wrinkled surface. Tears blurred her vision, and she blinked rapidly in a vain attempt to stem the flow. Bringing the age-old paper to her lips, she kissed the center spot, where the big seven lay.

"I just wish it could have been us," she murmured, choking on a sob.

Peering through her tears and the darkness, she took one last hard look at the ancient markings, to imprint them on her subconscious. To memorize them as a piece of her history with GT. But a cloud passed in front of the moon, obscuring them, and she was out of time. With a moan of frustration, she rolled the paper up into a small brown tube and, pulling the stopper out of the bottle, followed GT's strict instructions.

Swear! The word resounded against the churn of the waves.

"I swear," she whispered, putting the stopper back into the neck and tightening it securely. Pushing herself to a standing position, she brushed the sand from her skirt and lifted the bottle into her hands. The gentle breeze that had swept off the top of the water's surface picked up, buffeting her some as she gained her balance.

Running barefoot into the surf, she shivered as the frigid water sent a riot of gooseflesh cascading up her body. With one last look at the bottle that had managed to change her life irrevocably, she pressed it to her cheek and whispered, "Goodbye."

It took the last shred of strength she possessed to swing the bottle back, then hurl it as hard as she could into the whitecaps, where it landed with a plop, then…disappeared from sight. Hayley stood, ankle-deep in water, staring blankly out to sea, the way she was sure multitudes of women before her had done, wondering if—and when—her man would return.

As if in testament to the fact that her relationship with GT was well and truly over, black clouds like bearers of doom began to gallop wildly across the horizon, obliterating the moon's guiding light. The wind began to moan and howl a primitive banshee wail, and Hayley was suddenly chilled to the bone. A resounding clap of thunder rumbled off in the distance, then again louder and closer. Driving rain slanted down, almost as if the equestrian clouds, weary of their heavy burden, decided to rear back and set the deluge free.

The squall was as fierce as it was sudden. Searching the beach, she could see no signs of the teenagers that had been cavorting around the camp fire only moments ago. Suddenly frightened by the intensity of the strange storm, Hayley began to back up toward the shore. The wind whipped at her damp skirt, twisting it around her legs, and her hair, torn loose from its clip, stung her tear-streaked cheeks.

Struggling back to the spot where she'd left her purse and car keys, she turned one last time, facing nature's wrath, and looked out to sea. There wasn't a star in the sky now, and streaks of angry lightning rent the cloudy blackness.

Thunder cracked and rumbled, louder than she'd ever heard it before, and she knew that she had to leave. It wasn't safe for her to stay any longer, but unable to resist, she turned one last time and whispered, as the wind tore her words from her lips and flung them to the ends of the earth, "I loved you so much."

With those last words, she stumbled across the sand, her legs feeling suddenly too weak and rubbery to sustain her weight. It was almost as if she were moving in slow motion. Oh, she was tired. So very, very tired. And, for some reason, it seemed that the harder she ran, the slower she went.

A scream of frustration mixed with fear welled into her throat, but as much as she wanted to release it, she couldn't. Inching along at a snail's pace in the loose sand and blinding rain, Hayley wondered why running suddenly required so much effort. She knew she had to get away. To find safe haven. But she was so exhausted, and her legs simply wouldn't move fast enough.

The wind screamed in her ears, seeming to call her name as she sunk to the ground and rested her cheek on the sand's cool surface.

"Hayley..." came the haunting cry, "Hayley..."

Chapter Eleven

"Hayley." Hayley felt a warm hand grip her upper arm and give it a not-so-gentle shake. "*Hayley!* Cut it out, will you? For crying in the night, this is no time to clown around." Mercedes' nasal voice hissed low in her ear.

Slowly, ever so slowly, Hayley opened her eyes and looked around. What in heaven's name was she doing in the Technolabs Data Processing department? Raking her wild mass of curly hair away from her face, she sat up and looked around, completely dazed and disoriented.

"What's going on?" she mumbled. She felt as though she were surfacing from the kind of long sleep fairy tales were made of.

"You want to know what's going on?" Mercedes muttered under her breath, her head bobbing from side to side with exasperation, "I'll tell you what's going on. If you continue to catch up on your beauty sleep at your desk this way, you're going to get yourself canned." She folded her collar straight up and threw a colorful scarf around her neck. "Word has it that the new general manager of Technolabs just arrived on the property for his 'surprise' inspection.''

"He has?" Hayley asked dully as she blinked and looked around. Why wasn't any of this computing?

"Yes!" Mercedes huffed. "So look alive, will you? What'd you do? Stay up all night last night?"

Hayley frowned. "No...uh...no..." she said vaguely. "Mercedes, I just had the *weirdest* dream!"

"Oh, so that's what you've been doing all morning?" Mercedes rolled her eyes expressively. "And here I thought you were just demonstrating that idea you have about being able to do your job while in a coma with no discernible brainwave activity."

"No, really!" Hayley shook her head slightly to clear the cobwebs. "It was so real! You were in it! And my mom, and Mr. Peabody from Accounting and Mr. Franklin from Purchasing, and Mr. Tyrnan from Human Resources..." Her voice trailed off and her eyes glazed over with the memory. Had it really all just been a dream? The very idea was so deflating.

"Were Auntie Em and Toto there, too?" Mercedes laughed.

"Mercedes, I'm not kidding, it was the most amazing dream I've ever had."

"Oh, please. Any dream that stars Freddy the fruitcake and Ken the kinky is not my idea of amazing. Now, if you want to talk juicy, I had a dream the other night about Mel Gibson and Brad Pitt and they were fighting over me, and just as I was..." Mercedes stopped talking long enough to catch her breath—along with a glimpse of her friend's crumpled expression. "Oh, honey. What's the matter?"

Feeling incredibly idiotic as the tears brimmed in her eyes, Hayley ducked her head and searched her desktop for a tissue. Quickly dumping her purse out on the floor, she finally managed to locate a handkerchief and scrape most of her belongings back into her bag. She blinked rapidly in an attempt to stem the flow, but it was too late. One after the other, large tears spilled down her cheeks, soaking her lacy handkerchief.

"It was all just a dream. Ha," she squeaked, and shrugging, tried to laugh it off as some kind of temporary hormonal insanity.

Mercedes snagged the box of tissue from her own desktop and shoved it into Hayley's hands. "Here, honey. Mop it up. You want to look good for the new GM," she teased, trying to help.

"I don't care about the new GM," Hayley said grumpily, and blew her nose. Tilting her head back, she stared unseeing at the ceiling. "I just can't believe it was all just a dream. It was so real."

"Sounds more like a nightmare to me, considering all the people you said were in it." Mercedes crossed her eyes and stuck her tongue out dramatically. "I mean, Walt Tyrnan. Yuck. You're scraping the bottom of the barrel for things to cry about, kiddo. And you know what they say...."

"What?" Hayley sniffed, her smile quavering.

"You cry on your birthday, you cry all year long."

"Uh-oh." Her lower lip trembled uncontrollably. She sighed, glad that the walls of their partition shielded them from the curious stares of their co-workers. "In a way, you're right. Parts of it were nightmarish, yes. But, in another way, it was the most beautiful experience I've ever had." She glanced up at the puzzled look on her friend's face, and knew instinctively that Mercedes would never be able to understand the impact this dream had had on her very existence.

How did one begin to explain such a life-altering revelation? She wasn't the same person who'd fallen asleep at her desk that morning at all. Everything had changed. Most especially her outlook on the future. For now she knew that life didn't have to be a string of dreary events.

Life was what she made it. From now on, she would grab the brass ring. Go for the gusto. Throw her hat over the fence and see where it led her. And she would start by quitting her duller-than-dull job. Today.

A sudden commotion over at the other side of the Data Processing department drew their attention. The gratuitous fanfare could only signal one thing. The new general manager had arrived. Hayley slumped in her chair. If there was one thing she was not in the mood for, it was glad-handing some mucky-muck from above. Especially since this was her last day at Technolabs.

Ever loyal, Mercedes grabbed her makeup bag and dug out a compact and a lipstick. "Here, honey. Do something about your red nose."

Hayley looked down at the cosmetics her friend had thrust into her hands. *What the heck,* she thought, flipping open the compact and studying her reflection in the mirror. Might as well make a good impression while she was resigning. She dusted her nose with powder and quickly applied a light coat of lipstick. For good measure, she freshened her mascara and dragged a comb through her hair as the group of visiting dignitaries made the rounds.

Tossing the makeup bag back at Mercedes, Hayley haphazardly tidied her desk. No use going too crazy. She wouldn't be around after today, anyway. Staring at her monitor, she pretended to work, more for Mercedes' benefit than anything else.

Finally, the new head honcho and his entourage arrived at Hayley and Mercedes' cubicle and began making introductions. Walt Tyrnan from Human Resources crowded in between the two desks, his sunken chest puffed out most self-importantly. Ignoring him, Hayley continued typing.

"Ladies, this is our new general manager, Mr. Grant Thompson." Walt groped Hayley's shoulder and massaged it until she felt her skin begin to crawl. "Mr.

Thompson, I'd like you to meet two of our star data processors, Mercedes James and Hayley Douglas."

Star data processor. That was a laugh, Hayley thought, slipping the completed document into her Out basket. Well, not for long, Walt old boy, she reflected, extracting her shoulder from his clammy grip as she spun in her chair to greet the new GM. Just as soon as she could tender her resignation, she was blowing this popsicle stand.

Or not.

Her pulse roared in her ears, louder—if possible—than the thunder from the beach of her dream. She felt suddenly light-headed as her eyes slammed into the most beautiful midnight gaze she'd ever dreamed of.

GT!

"M...M...Mr. *Thompson?*" she stammered.

Like the static undercurrent of a tropical storm, the sparks literally crackled between them. "Please, I...prefer to be called GT." Mr. Thompson held out his hand, his eyes narrowing slightly. "Have we met before?"

"I...uh..." Hayley shrugged helplessly. How did one explain to one's new general manager that they had lived together for the past two weeks? No, no, technically they'd lived together for the next two weeks, but she was too thunderstruck to split hairs.

"I have the most incredible sense of déjà vu right now," he said, grasping her hand in his and looking deeply into her eyes with a probing intensity that made her blush. He winked lazily at her, with that same old heart-stoppingly sexy wink of his she'd come to know and love. "You ever get that?"

"Yes," she breathed, smiling up into his fabulously handsome face. He looked exactly the same. He smelled exactly the same. He felt exactly the same. He sounded exactly the same. Deciding that this was neither the time nor place to discover if he tasted exactly the same, Hayley just stood, gazing up at, and inhaling, and grasping the hand of . . . her genie.

Bending down, he retrieved a small brown piece of paper off the floor and glanced at it with a thoughtful frown. "I can't get over the uncanny feeling of . . . of—" he traced the center of the paper with his finger, then studied the designs at the edges "—familiarity." Shaking his head, he handed her the scrap. "Is this yours?"

"Oh." Hayley glanced at the floor, embarrassed. "I was just cleaning out my purse earlier and I..." Her eyes strayed to the paper he'd handed her, and her voice trailed off as the conversation went on around her.

Walt grabbed Mr. Thompson's arm and tugged him toward Mercedes. "This is Mercedes," he said huskily, groping her co-worker's shoulder.

That was it! The piece of parchment that she'd found on the beach later that afternoon...or whenever, she thought, bending her brain around the time warp that constituted her relationship with GT. Smoothing the paper out on her desktop, she bent over it and gasped audibly. The big seven was . . . *gone!*

She glanced up at GT, then back down at the paper. The galaxies and planets were still there, happily in their orbits, and the disasters, natural and unnatural, seemed untouched, as well. Everything was there but the seven small sevens.

And . . . *the one big seven.*

It was then she remembered GT's words.

"If I could figure out a way to stay with you, and love you, without breaking my vows, I would do it in a heartbeat. I would give anything, including my life, to be with you forever. But, honey, dammit, I made a vow...."

She stared at the blank spot on the paper. What did this mean? Was this Mortimer's secret? Could *she* have made his vows null and void with one giant wish? Was that why the planet was still rotating? Was that why she could remember him? Was that why he couldn't seem to remember her? And more important, would he remember her if he fell in love with her as a mortal?

Questions raced though her deliriously happy mind with the speed of a lightning flash. She only knew that GT wouldn't be back unless he had wanted it as much as she did. Unless he loved her as much as she loved him. Because, if what he'd told her before was true, he'd given up his job, his future and his life to be standing there with her at this moment.

Overwhelmed at the price he'd paid, she felt tears of joy prick the backs of her eyes. Blinking them away, she suddenly realized that she'd been standing with her mouth open, staring at the piece of parchment, for quite a while. Hayley straightened and, lifting her head, watched as GT made small talk with Mercedes.

When they were finished, GT stepped back toward Hayley. "Forgive me if this sounds like some kind of a bad pickup line, but I'm sure we've met before. And it's going to drive me crazy until I figure out where." He folded his arms across his broad chest and regarded her *King and I*-style. "Why don't you and Mercedes join us for lunch? A little birdie just told me it's your birthday." He grinned over at Mercedes, who shrugged impishly. He glanced down at his watch. "And since I'm implementing a new policy about the birthday lunch, we may as well start with you. I need to talk to you two, anyway. Regarding your job descriptions." With a light hand at the small of her back, he gestured for her to come along with him and his group down the hallway.

"Oh, well, sure, uh, what about our jobs?" Hayley asked, suddenly nervous. What had he heard about her lackadaisical job performance? She didn't want to get fired now that she'd finally met the man of her dreams.

"Oh, nothing major. I read them over last week and they just seem a little dull to me, that's all. I thought we could talk about putting a little creativity and adventure into your day.'' He smiled down at her. ''I find that makes for a self-confident employee. Work shouldn't be boring. It should be fun.''

''It should?'' Hayley breathed, more in love with him now than ever before.

''Absolutely,'' he said, shrugging loosely and casting a sidelong wink in her direction. ''You've got to have a laugh or two along the way, or it's just not worth it.''

As they strode along, moving apart from the rest of the group, Hayley could feel his eyes scrutinizing her curiously.

''Okay,'' he said, and grinned smugly. ''I've got it. McKinley Elementary, Mrs. Woods's second-grade class. Right?'' He touched her elbow, responding to a magnetic pull over which he felt curiously powerless. He'd never felt this way before.

Hayley stared up at him, puzzled. ''Pardon?''

''No?'' As they moved down the hallway, GT racked his brain, trying to discover where he'd met this vision of loveliness before. He would figure it out eventually. Because if there was one thing he knew from the split second he'd laid eyes on her only moments ago, sooner or later, she would be his wife. He scratched his temple, feeling bemused. ''Hmm,'' he mused, holding the door open for her as they exited the building. ''Cal State, Biology 101?''

Hayley giggled. ''No.''

''Swim team at Olinger swimming pool? The Dairy Queen at Seventh and Market? No? Did you happen to attend the big New Year's Eve party at Mortimer Eugene's place? Nah,'' he said with a slight shake of his head, ''I'd have remembered you.''

''You're sure about that?'' Hayley's bubbly laughter echoed in the empty hallway as the door swung shut, and GT's persistent voice wafted back, growing dim now as they moved into their future together.

"Do you believe in love at first sight?"

Hayley's voice shimmered with happiness. "Well, I think I'm more of a believer in love at seventh sight...."

Later that afternoon, after she'd finally caught up on all the work she'd slept through, Hayley ambled tiredly across the Technolabs parking lot to her car. It had been an incredibly long, emotionally draining day. The only bright spots since waking up at her desk that morning were her birthday lunch and the half-dozen or so times she'd managed to catch a glimpse of GT as he was being ushered around by Walt. She was still far too dazed and confused by everything that had happened to her that day to even begin to try to analyze it.

Unfortunately, in spite of her amazing dream that morning, nothing had changed on her social docket for the evening. Everyone, it seemed, was still too busy to help her celebrate her twenty-seventh birthday. And GT still didn't seem to remember her. An acute sense of loss—over something she couldn't be sure she'd ever even had—settled over her.

Unlocking and opening Old Trusty's door, she was hit full in the face by intense heat as she slid into the stifling interior. When she attempted to start her engine she was greeted by a peculiar—and all too familiar—sputter and buzz. She let her head fall back against the searing upholstery of her seat and groaned. It figured. Just her luck. Old Trusty had finally given up.

Hoisting herself out of her car, she glanced hopefully around the parking lot for someone to assist her. It soon became painfully clear that everyone had already left.

"For crying out loud," she yelled in futility, and shot a baleful look down at her pumps. "I don't want to walk all the way home in high heels. Why me? Why on my birthday of all days?" She flopped miserably across the hood of her car and moaned. "Damn," she whimpered, fighting the urge to lie down on the hot pavement and throw a tantrum over life's little injustices. "I just wish I had a ride home."

Sounds of a car pulling to a stop behind her brought her head up. The smoothly purring engine of a high performance foreign import idled quietly as GT rolled down his window and grinned.

"You know," he said, winking that heart-stoppingly sexy wink of his, "I had a feeling that Old Trusty was going to conk out on you today."

As she stared at him, her jaw slack with wonder, sheer, unadulterated joy bubbled up into Hayley's throat. "You did?" she breathed, barely daring to hope that her dreams were about to come true.

"Uh-huh," he said with a smile. Reaching over, he opened the passenger door of his sports car. "Get in. I want to take you out to dinner. To celebrate your birthday, among other things."

Hayley hastened to obey. "Nice car." She grinned and slid into the cool interior, remembering the first time she'd taken a ride with him.

Returning her grin, he leaned across her lap and helped her with the complex seat belt. "It's no magic carpet, but it sure beats taking a taxi." The belt—and their gazes— locked. They sat for a long moment like that, him leaning across her, a supercharged awareness crackling between them.

Hayley slowly released her breath. "Does this mean what I think it means?"

His smiling eyes searched hers. "That I've fallen head over heels in love with you?"

"Yes." The whispered word was a prayer.

"Yes." Slowly, with great reverence for the solemnity of the occasion, he nodded. "The big seven was Mortimer's loophole."

"You're here because of the big seven?"

"It was my dream—to come back to you. And when you threw my bottle into the water, you gave me the chance to be human—to love you the way you deserve. I don't know how my bosses did it, but I'm now a mortal man."

Hayley's eyes shimmered with hope and happiness. "When did you remember you were GT?"

Cupping her cheek in his hand, he stroked its smooth surface with his thumb. "I think it hit me, oh . . . about the half-dozenth time I found an excuse to pass your desk this afternoon." He touched his lips to hers and smiled against them. "Came to me like a bolt of lightning," he murmured, and pulled her mouth to his for a lingering kiss.

She clung to him, realizing with a sweet poignancy the sacrifice he was making for her. The wild joy she suddenly felt knew no bounds. He was here, and he was hers. What an incredible gift. And just in time for her birthday. She shivered with excitement, impatient to share her good news with her mother and Mercedes. They would be so happy for her.

Pulling slightly back, Hayley leaned against his embrace, a pensive frown marring her brow. Then again, just what would her mother and Mercedes make of this? Undoubtedly they would wonder why she was jumping into a relationship with a man that—to them— would seem to be a complete stranger, not to mention her new boss. "GT?" She drew her lower lip between her teeth.

"Hmm?" he asked, nibbling that sensitive spot beneath her jaw.

"People will surely find out about us...being in love and all. What do you think they'll say?" she wondered, gasping as he rained a trail of kisses from her jaw to her chin.

"Who cares?" Reaching up, GT pushed a lock of hair away from her face before bestowing a gentle kiss on the tip of her nose. His dark eyes danced with mischievous charm. "Probably, when they get over the initial surprise, they'll say, Looks like she finally got her wish."

Hayley smiled and twined her fingers into the midnight blackness of his hair. ''And,'' she murmured against his mouth, ''they'd be right.''

*　*　*　*　*

Take 4 bestselling love stories FREE

Plus get a FREE surprise gift!

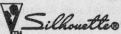

As seen on TV!

Free Gift Offer

With a Free Gift proof-of-purchase from any Silhouette® book,
you can receive a beautiful cubic zirconia pendant.

This gorgeous marquise-shaped stone is a genuine cubic
zirconia—accented by an 18" gold tone necklace.

(Approximate retail value $19.95)

Send for yours today...

compliments of ▼ *Silhouette*®

To receive your free gift, a cubic zirconia pendant, send us one original proof-of-
purchase, photocopies not accepted, from the back of any Silhouette Romance™,
Silhouette Desire®, Silhouette Special Edition®, Silhouette Intimate Moments®
or Silhouette Yours Truly™ title available in August, September or October at your favorite
retail outlet, together with the Free Gift Certificate, plus a check or money order for
$1.65 U.S./$2.15 CAN. (do not send cash) to cover postage and handling, payable
to Silhouette Free Gift Offer. We will send you the specified gift. Allow 6 to 8 weeks for
delivery. Offer good until October 31, 1996 or while quantities last. Offer valid in the
U.S. and Canada only.

Free Gift Certificate

Name: _____

Address: _____

City: _____ State/Province: _____ Zip/Postal Code: _____

Mail this certificate, one proof-of-purchase and a check or money order for postage
and handling to: SILHOUETTE FREE GIFT OFFER 1996. In the U.S.: 3010 Walden
Avenue, P.O. Box 9077, Buffalo NY 14269-9077. In Canada: P.O. Box 613, Fort Erie,
Ontario L2Z 5X3.

FREE GIFT OFFER   084-KMD
ONE PROOF-OF-PURCHASE
To collect your fabulous FREE GIFT, a cubic zirconia pendant, you must include this
original proof-of-purchase for each gift with the properly completed Free Gift Certificate.

084-KMD

You can run, but you cannot hide...from love.

This August, experience danger, excitement and love on the run with three couples thrown together by life-threatening circumstances.

Enjoy three complete stories by some of your favorite authors—all in one special collection!

THE PRINCESS AND THE PEA
by Kathleen Korbel

IN SAFEKEEPING
by Naomi Horton

FUGITIVE
by Emilie Richards

Available this August wherever books are sold.

SREQ896

Fortune's Children™

Bestselling Author
LISA JACKSON

Continues the twelve-book series—FORTUNE'S CHILDREN
in August 1996 with Book Two

THE MILLIONAIRE AND THE COWGIRL

When playboy millionaire Kyle Fortune inherited a Wyoming
ranch from his grandmother, he never expected to come
face-to-face with Samantha Rawlings, the willful woman
he'd never forgotten…and the daughter he'd never known.
Although Kyle enjoyed his jet-setting life-style, Samantha and
Caitlyn made him yearn for hearth and home.

MEET THE FORTUNES—a family whose legacy is greater than
riches. Because where there's a will…there's a *wedding!*

A CASTING CALL TO
ALL FORTUNE'S CHILDREN FANS!
If you are truly one of the fortunate
few, you may win a trip to
Los Angeles to audition for
Wheel of Fortune®. Look for
details in all retail Fortune's Children titles!

WHEEL OF FORTUNE is a registered trademark of Califon Productions, Inc.©
1996 Califon Productions, Inc. All Rights Reserved.

Look us up on-line at: http://www.romance.net

FC-2-C-R

Coming this August
from Silhouette Romance

Expanding upon our popular Fabulous Fathers series, these irresistable heros are going even farther beyond daddy duty... for the love of children and unforgettable heroines!

UNDERCOVER DADDY
by
Lindsay Longford
(SR#1168, August)

Detective Walker Ford had always loved Kate McDaniels, but she'd married his best friend. Now she was widowed with an infant son—and they desperately needed his help. Walker had sworn to protect the baby with his life—but who would protect his heart from the boy's beautiful mother?

Don't miss this Super Fabulous Father—only in

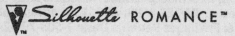
Silhouette ROMANCE™

Look us up on-line at: http://www.romance.net

SFF896

You're About to Become a

Privileged Woman

Reap the rewards of fabulous free gifts and benefits with proofs-of-purchase from Silhouette and Harlequin books

Pages & Privileges™

It's our way of thanking you for buying our books at your favorite retail stores.

PROOF OF PURCHASE
SR-PP163
Offer expires October 31, 1996

Pages & Privileges ™

**Harlequin and Silhouette—
the most privileged readers in the world!**

For more information about Harlequin and Silhouette's PAGES & PRIVILEGES program call the Pages & Privileges Benefits Desk: 1-503-794-2499

Silhouette®

SR-PP163